Thunder Moon

MAX BRAND

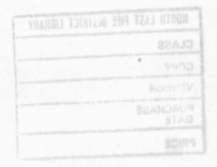

SEVERN HOUSE

This 1979 edition from
SEVERN HOUSE PUBLISHERS LTD
144–146 New Bond Street, London W1Y 9FD.

First published in the U.K. by Hodder & Stoughton 1970

ISBN 0 7278 0443 x

Brand, Max
    Thunder moon.
    I. Title
    823'.9'1F   PS3511.A87T/

ISBN 0-7278-0443-X

Printed in Great Britain by litho at
The Anchor Press Ltd and bound by
Wm Brendon & Son Ltd, both of
Tiptree, Essex

"This very day," his foster father said, "young Waiting Bear is to have his breasts opened with the knife and the thongs passed through them. You and I shall go up with him. I shall cut your breasts with the knife. I shall pass the thongs through the cuts. There will be a little blood and a little pain. But afterward, when you come back to my tepee, the mark of your manhood will be upon your body for the whole tribe to know that you are worthy to be a brave, and Tarawa will be ready to welcome another warrior."

So Thunder Moon climbed up the hill, pale, but with his jaw resolutely set.

"They are watching. We cannot wait any longer!" Big Hard Face cautioned, and at the same time he gripped the flesh over the right breast of Thunder Moon and drew it stiffly out from his body. The knife was raised and flashed. The brightness of it burned into the very soul of Thunder Moon. Then a pang of exquisite agony pierced his body—to the very heart, it seemed to him. His throat muscles unlocked. And a scream of terror burst from his lips!

Chapter One

First of all, before anything else is attempted, you must understand that December means Big Hard Face, just as November is called simply Hard Face by the Cheyennes.

As a rule such names have nothing to do with the appearance of an Indian. They have a moral, a sentimental, or most of all a purely incidental significance, and may be picked up in anything from a swimming match to a battle. And as a matter of fact, Big Hard Face was not called by that grim name because he was ugly. His naming was a matter which had to do with the untimely month in which he was born, the very last month of the year, when the vast prairies were covered with wind-furrowed snows.

Three or four other children were born into that group of the tribe in the same month, but they all died, because the winter mortality among the plains Indians used to be a fearful thing. But Big Hard Face, or December, as it may be better to call him, lived through the winter and grew fat and boisterous in the warm spring suns, to the delight of his parents and of the whole tribe. Because so many others had been taken during his infancy, it was felt that their lost good fortunes in war and in peace might accompany the new boy.

Big Hard Face did not disappoint the good prophets. There was only one serious mishap in all of his early life, and that was when he was six years old. The colt which he was riding bucked him off and then trampled across his face. They picked up December with his face an indistinguishable mass of blood and disarranged gristle and bone. Thereafter, above the eyes, he was as likely an Indian as you could ever wish to see, and if you watched him wrapped almost to the forehead in his buffalo robe, when he had gained manhood, you would have picked him as the handsomest of his entire tribe.

But when the robe was removed from the lower part of his face, you changed your mind, be sure, with much speed. For Big Hard Face wore a dismal mask that had very little relation to a human countenance. Here and there you could make out something that should be a human feature. That was the chin, surely, that lopsided thing. And the broad, misshapen slit was the mouth, of course. The nose was not in evidence, but he breathed through two smashed holes. And all the good copper of his skin was altered and slashed across with white hollows and sharp white ridges of scar tissue.

The Pawnees are a brawny and hard-minded race of fellows, but it is creditably reported that when they saw Big Hard Face charging, that ghastly slab of a face distorted with a war cry, a band of fifty of them had taken to their heels and fled for their lives, convinced that the devil in person was after them.

However, beauty is not everything.

Big Hard Face, or December, was strong, brave, and silent, as a youth. He listened when the old men talked. And so, in turn, men were willing to listen to him when he wished to make himself heard.

As he grew older, he counted no fewer than seven *coups,* and he was known to have slain with his own hand five enemies in full battle, and their scalps dried in his tepee. Such feats of arms were not unaccompanied by other manifestations of worth. He was generous, giving freely of those things which he had about him. His lodge was open to the poor and the sick. Among the braves of the tribe, he was not boastful except when it became a good Cheyenne, for the sake of his tribe, and to impress lessons of Indian virtue upon the younger tribesmen.

But with all of this, he had such goods wits, and he knew so eminently well how to use them, that he was able to amass a considerable fortune. He had a fine herd of horses, all selected ponies, and his clothes, and robes, and his household equipment in general, were such as even a chief would have been proud to own.

There was, however, a flaw in his life and in his fortune. It was to be noticed that whereas the other middle-aged braves among the Cheyennes frequently went out to watch the games of the children, or to see the boys racing, or swimming, or wrestling, Big Hard Face was never to be seen in such assemblies.

And often, when it was necessary for him to pass through a group of the boys, he would draw a fold of his buffalo robe across his face.

People wondered at this, but there were some of the oldest and the wisest men in the tribe who understood. For Big Hard Face, as he drew toward the end of middle age and his marriageable days, was without children to honor his declining years. And for children, and above all for a son, he yearned with a mighty passion.

Woe to the man who cannot keep a woman in his house, for he will go all his life with the fear of death staring in his face, and no comfort in his prospect.

So there were no children in the lodge of poor December. It was in vain that he had thrice married. Thrice he had paid a high price for a wife, and thrice, he had treated her with all the kindness of which he was capable, and he was above all a kind man. Yet in each case within a month or two, one day he came home and found his lodge empty.

His home was cared for by an aunt, an old woman with a crooked back but with hands as capable as the hands of a man, and wonderfully skilled in cookery.

She filled the lodge, but she did not fill the heart of poor December. And it was after the lodge had for the third time known the presence of a wife, and had for the third time been emptied, that Big Hard Face turned his head from his people and went off by himself in the wild ocean of the plains. Because he knew that if he remained among his people, the women would smile when they passed him.

After each of these un-marriages, he had gone forth and performed a deed worth relating. Now he was determined to perform a feat greater than any that he had ever attempted before, though what it might be, he hardly was able to determine.

However, when he left the village and started on his voyage with two traveling ponies and a running horse of the finest, he set his face toward that point of the compass where the greatest and the strangest dangers might be expected.

The Cheyennes were now encamped on the most southerly and easternmost extremity of their range, and Big Hard Face aimed his course still farther south and east.

He did not ask advice before he started on his journey. He made his own medicine, and the sign it gave him was good, and so he started upon the inland voyage leisurely, as one prepared to take his time over a great distance, and keep his horses in excellent condition for a swift retreat, pursued by the enemy.

What that enemy might be, he only realized dimly.

Now and then he had had to do with cunning, sharp-minded white traders for the buffalo robes which were dressed in his lodge. But there were tales of a vast country to the East where the white faces roamed as thick as the buffalo themselves, and he had heard tales of cities into which the whole Cheyenne nation might be poured. He knew that these stories were lies, because it was certain that the Cheyennes were the favorites of the Sky People, and the greatest and most powerful and warlike race on earth. Nevertheless, it would be well to see what the truth about the white man was.

And above all, it would be well to return with a white scalp.

He left the treeless plains; he journeyed across green lands. Rivers grew more frequent. Rain clouds hung heavy in the sky, the heat and the humidity grew oppressive. And the new moon which had watched him from the edge of the western sky when he departed had now passed through three phases.

And then he came to a region of cultivated fields. There were houses everywhere, and the barking of dogs surrounded him, day and night, and the crowing of roosters like thin trumpets prophesying danger. He gave up travel beneath the sun. He went forward only in the hours of darkness, feeling his way from point to point.

He saw strange sights in this land, as he crept forward out of the forest after sunset and came close to the verge of towns where the lodges of the warriors were built of stone and of wood, and where myriads of lights gleamed from the tepees. And a dozen times he had a deed presented to his hand, when he came in the woods upon single wanderers, or groups of two or three—all so high headed and unsuspecting of danger that he could have butchered them, and taken their scalps.

But still he held his hand, for he had not yet found a deed suited to his mind. Just what that deed should be, he had no idea, but he felt some great thing growing to fruition within his heart, and he was willing to wait until the voice of God told him what to do.

Now Big Hard Face traveled late one night, and the next morning when he wakened he was on the edge of a wood, and beyond the wood there was a green lawn, and beyond the lawn there was a great lodge, all built of brick and wood, and three columns of smoke came from its roof, and there was a sense of many people within. In the fields near by, there roamed such horses as he had never seen before—horses long of leg and gaunt of belly and mighty of heart and long of neck, horses which looked to have the speed of the wind.

They were fenced in, but the fence ran deep into the edge of the wood, and in the heat of the day the horses came there to rest. He went closer to watch. He went closer still. He had a vast desire to touch these glimmering creatures, and when he showed himself, they did not whirl away and flee. They merely raised their heads and watched him out of great, kind eyes.

So the soul of Big Hard Face grew hungrier and hungrier.

There were a score of these animals. With a faultless instinct, he chose a glorious stallion, a rich, dark chestnut. It submitted to his touch, and his lariat, merely sniffing curiously at the unfamiliar odors on his clothes. He took this treasure through the bars and away among the trees and there his hands went ceaselessly over the wonderful horse, until he had seen it with the tips of his fingers, like a blind man.

But one horse grows old and dies.

He went back. How should he choose, where all were flawless? But he picked at last three mares, beautiful as music, gentle past belief. He led them into the woods, also, and began to wait impatiently for night.

He did not know that the crowning feat of all was still to come.

Chapter Two

That day grew old slowly.

The horses moved from the tree shadows into the warm middle of the pasture, again, and began to crop the thick, short grass, or to play with one another like happy children. But their beauty did not tempt Big Hard Face very greatly. He only wanted the darkness to begin, so that he could flee west and north with his four godlike prizes.

He went from one to the other. If they could not understand his words of good Cheyenne, they could at least understand the rich softness of his voice, and they pricked their ears to it. They cropped the grass beneath the trees contentedly. All their lives they had learned that man may be trusted implicitly, and this, though he wore a skin of a different color, was a man. Even the stallion did not neigh!

Roaming restlessly to the verge of the woods, again, thinking of the four, to the backs of which he had already transferred his saddle and his packs, Big Hard Face saw a tall young white man come out from the house with a young white squaw walking beside him. How wonderful would her masses of long golden hair appear, hanging in his tepee! And the black locks of this young stalwart, they would make a worthy scalp, also.

Big Hard Face nursed the butt of his rifle with eager hands.

But still he hesitated. Courage is great in the heart of every worthy Indian, but caution is still more highly prized, and he that ventures neck for nothing is only a fool.

Now if the gun spoke in this peaceful clearing, would not many people begin to come at once, carrying guns? And before he could take the scalps or even count the *coups,* bullets would be flying about him. He would be lost, and his fine selected horses would be lost to his tribe.

He sighed, and watching the golden hair, he sighed again, and still more bitterly.

A nurse came from the house behind the pair. Big Hard Face saw her of the golden hair lift a baby from the arms of its nurse, then toss it and fondle it. And the laughter of the baby floated cheerfully across the air and fell like sad music on the heart of the Indian. In his tepee there were no such voices!

He watched the young pair pass on; he saw the nurse bring the child to the shadow of a great old apple tree and there she stripped it and laid it on its back on a blanket to kick its fat legs in the dapple of sun and shade and throw up its tiny fists and laugh and gurgle with a perfect freedom and a perfect delight.

It was a glorious specimen of man child. Even its white skin was hardly a blemish in the eyes of Big Hard Face. In his dreams, such a child had often come to him.

He found himself beyond the verge of the trees hardly knowing how he had been drawn there, until the nurse chanced to turn and see him.

Her scream went tingling through the air; she fled as fast as her heavy legs could carry her toward the house, and Big Hard Face, startled back to his senses, suddenly heard the voice of his God speaking to him. This was the great deed for which he had been drawn so far from his people!

He caught up the baby with a sweep of his hand,

snatched the blanket around it, and bounded back into the shadow of the trees, and into the saddle on the stallion, and then softly rode north and west.

He heard shrill voices behind him, but they ceased, and the kind silence of the woods followed. The baby in his arm was striking at his face and laughing, and every blow of the soft little hands touched the heart of the Cheyenne. The son of his lodge was beating him. In the speech of the Cheyennes it would call him "father."

So, in a gap of the woods, he halted the stallion and raised his face to the blue heavens above, darkening toward evening time, while he gave thanks to the Sky People for their gift to him.

After that, he rode on again, secure, but watchful.

He came to a road, laid straight and true through the woodland and across the dusky fields. While he waited there, a band of a dozen riders rushed past. Their strained faces and their foaming horses told their story—they were on his trail. But Big Hard Face laughed. Heaven does not recall its gifts from a good Indian!

As the twilight deepened, the baby began to cry, fretfully. It was hungry, then; and the Sky People told Big Hard Face what to do.

He slipped into a field and found a fat-sided cow waiting at the bars. One blow killed her; then with a dexterous knife he cut away the udder and brought it to the boy, and held the little one on his lap and offered a teat.

"Oh-ho!" murmured Big Hard Face. "Do you understand me? This is my first gift, but not my last to you, my son. Drink deep. The warpath lies ahead for you and me. What scalps shall dry above your fire! When the days of Big Hard Face are dark, you shall rise like a second sun to warm his cold blood. Drink deep! I shall not fail you, boy, and you will not fail me hereafter!"

That strange dinner was finished and the baby yawned and curled up for sleep, and Big Hard Face held him close, and breathed gently.

It was utter dark when he started on again, and in the distance there was the baying of dogs. He did not know but he had heard that the white men train dogs to follow both man and horse. Therefore he began to ride fast.

He held to his way as though he had a lodestone to guide him, but he shifted first to a ten-mile stretch of the highway and then cut across another ten miles of smooth meadow, and again, before the morning, he was winding through woodland. He swam his horses across a shallow, easy-flowing river, and made on again from the farther bank.

There was no noise of dogs behind him, now.

In the morning, the child cried again. It had cried before, during that long ride, from the misery of its hard position on the arm of its foster father. But now it was hungry, and another cow died that the boy might eat. While the Cheyenne rested his horses, he made a little contrivance of fence boards and bands of buffalo hide such as Indian mothers carried upon their backs, in his tribe, as a sort of portable cradle for their children.

Before he had finished, he could hear the wavering voices of a pack of hounds crying on the horizon, and he knew that the pursuit was creeping up on him again. So he placed the child in the new conveyance, strapped it across his back, and with saddle transferred to the strongest-looking of the three mares, and the other horses led by rawhide lariats, he began to follow the northern and western trail again.

Perhaps all would have gone well if he had had only to deal with such powers as men possessed on the prairies, but it was different in this region. The whole country had become alarmed, it seemed. He found excited little bands of hunters everywhere. Three times he was chased that second day, and three times a lucky shot from his rifle dropped a horse beneath a pursuer and made the others fall back. But it was a wretched day, for the child at his back wailed tirelessly all the while. And every cry was like death to Big Hard Face. Better for it to die, however, than for him to abandon the gift of the Sky People.

So he kept on his way, and as he rode, he saw the end of the cultivated fields, and before him began the broad edges of the prairie once more.

He gave thanks, like a sailor who enters upon familiar seas. No dogs ever bred could catch him now, and let the horses follow if they could! They would need more skill on the trail than white men were fabled to have!

For a week he rode cautiously, and twice a day he delayed his journey to lay elaborate trail problems, such as even the keen nose and fathomless wits of grizzly would have found it hard to unravel. But those who followed Big Hard Face must have worked at these things in vain, for he was troubled no longer. Yet he maintained a terrible pace for a week. And in that time he covered as much ground on these long-legged speedsters as he had covered in three times that number of days coming down the out trail.

For a terrible anxiety harassed him.

The child which had been so fat and rosy when he found it, was now thin and pale, and there was a crease between its eyes; its hands trembled and were almost transparent, and its lips quivered even in its sleep, and its voice wailed ceaselessly through every waking hour.

He killed what he could of mother antelope and deer and gave it to suckle. But the ardors of the long ride, perhaps, were what were killing the youngster.

A hundred times a day, Big Hard Face cast anguished eyes up to the sky, and the people who surely dwell there, asking them if they would take away the gift which they had so lately given to him? And then he would struggle on, riding the horses to the verge of death.

They had been sleek and gay when he found them; they were four stumbling skeletons when, on a day, he saw smoke rising out of the morning sky, and sent his animals at a staggering gallop over the hills and down toward his village. God had been good to him, and the tribe had not moved during all his absence.

A screaming crowd of boys, naked on their ponies, raced about him like sparrows before a swooping hawk. He heeded them not. He rushed on through the long street of the village to his own tepee and sprang to the ground.

There was his aunt, but she would not do.

Green Antelope stood gaping at the flap of her lodge, a baby at her breast. He strode to her, pushed her own child away, and gave her his gift from heaven.

"I have five horses waiting for you in my herd, Green Antelope. Will you keep this son of mine until his teeth can bite meat?"

Chapter Three

If Big Hard Face had been considered an eminent warrior and a wholly desirable member of the community before, he was now raised to the rank of the leading heroes of the tribe. In the eyes of the Cheyenne, it would have been hard to choose which point of the feats of December had been most admirable—the length of his solitary journey; the strange sights which he had seen and the narratives he could make of them which held even the professional story-tellers in awe; or the quartet of magnificent horses which he had brought back; or, finally, the manchild which he had brought to raise in his lodge until he became a warrior to fight for the Cheyenne nation!

All of these items were sufficiently miraculous, and by the common voice of the nation, it was decided that Big Hard Face was a man unquestionably under the protection of the Sky People. They had devised his wifeless and childless existence, just so that they could give him with their own hands a son of their own creation.

For such the white boy was felt to be, and great things were prophesied for his future. There was only one sour face and one ugly voice, and that was raised by White Crow, the aunt of Big Hard Face himself.

She looked with no favor upon the newcomer in the lodge when the baby was brought there after it had been weaned.

"A good name does not make a brave warrior," she

declared, "and though you name him Cheyenne, the color of his skin will always call you a liar."

Big Hard Face was not a man of violence, but now he seized a stick, and shook it vehemently.

"She-coyote!" he called her. "You have snarled at me for many years. But if you snarl at him, the Sky People will tell me to break all your bones!"

So she held her tongue when she was before her stalwart nephew, but among the other women of the tribe her tongue would never stop wagging.

After all, the boy had mighty faults. He grew taller than his compatriots of the same age, and somewhat bigger, especially about the shoulders, but what is the flesh when the spirit is lacking? And it was greatly to be feared that the spirit in this child was not all that could be wished.

He was a crying baby, and he grew up into a tearful child. If he stubbed his toe, or barked his shins, or bumped his head, he would sit down in the dust and rock his sunbrowned body back and forth and wail until his voice was singing like an echo in the farthest corner of the camp.

The chief medicine man was one day speaking with Big Hard Face—that was in the sixth year of the white child's life—and he had been called in to help find a name for the adopted son of December.

"Look!" said Big Hard Face. "There he stands, yonder, and he is taller than all the others except for the son of Three Buffalo. Find me a good name for him, to help him to be a good man!"

The medicine man watched and said nothing until there was a sudden scuffle, and a lithe little Indian lad, gripping the son of Big Hard Face, rolled him head over heels in the dust.

The boy sat up and shook the dust out of his long black hair, howling enormously.

"Did you not get him in the time when the horses grow fat and there is thunder in the sky?" the medicine man asked.

"Yes," admitted Big Hard Face.

"Then," said the medicine man rather maliciously, "I should advise you to call him Thunder Moon, because he makes a great noise!"

This was an obvious stroke of satire, but nevertheless, though Big Hard Face was angered at the time, he was afterward delighted with the connotation of the name. It called up in his mind a picture of whole hosts of Pawnees fleeing before the dreadful hand of his white son.

"Thunder Moon!"

So would they flee before the thunder and the lightning of the Sky People!

Accordingly, he took the suggestion, though he denied its implications in the mind of the suggester. And "Thunder Moon" was the name ceremoniously bestowed upon the youngster.

Ordinarily, the names which parents choose for their children in an Indian tribe do not stick. But some witty nickname, or some piece of sarcasm will cling like tar in its place. For there is a considerable streak of sharpness in the nature of a red, and he likes the word which cuts. For that very reason the tribe was pleased to accept the name Thunder Moon—not because of what it meant to the celebrated brave, Big Hard Face, but because of what had been in the mind of the medicine man.

And now, as the years went by, it was very clear that Thunder Moon was no hero, in the ordinary acceptance of the word. Neither was he a very clever lad. Before long, it was well known throughout the tribe that Big Hard Face had been given by the Sky People a fool to raise in his empty lodge, and there were many sarcastic smiles devoted to that subject.

We may add up the trying defects of Thunder Moon as they revealed themselves to the critical minds of the elders of the Cheyenne tribe.

Granting, in the first place, that the boy was big and well made, and promised to be still better proportioned when he reached manhood, yet he was astonishingly awkward, and what is strength without grace, in a race of horsemen?

He learned all things slowly.

Boys of six rode far better than he could at eight, and swam farther and faster, and ran more lightly and swiftly and with more endurance. He could not strike the mark with a play bow, and his efforts with a knife were simply pitiful to behold. He could not throw an ax, and when he strove to leap and imitate the war dance, the Cheyenne elders bowed their heads to keep Big Hard Face from seeing their smiles.

But worst of all, when it came to the mimic combat of wrestling, where boys should first learn to struggle as with an enemy, Thunder Moon was simply ridiculous. The agile young Cheyennes were able to lay him on his back before the game had well begun.

Still worse than that, he always resented his fall.

And when the boys laughed to see him down, he took it as a personal insult and would draw apart, to brood by himself. Indeed, as time went on, he led a more and more lonely existence. He was much with his adopted father, and he was much with the horses of his father's herd.

They had grown into a tidy little band, by this time, most of them with a broad blaze of white on the forehead, like the stallion which was their ancestor, and the hearts of the other Cheyennes were sore with envy when they saw this clumsy boy on the back of some peerless charger, careering across the plains.

They scorned him all the more for it. Because he did not conquer his horses by hardy strength and daring and cruelty; he wooed and won them, and petted them until they trusted him, and then he would venture his precious bones on their backs. How much nobler, then, to see any other Cheyenne boy spring upon the bare back of an unbroken pony and ride it while it struggled as though to buck its skin over its head!

There was no nobleness in Thunder Moon. As he grew taller and more awkward, he grew also more shamefaced. He drew more and more apart. Even Big Hard Face began to have a few doubts, though he would never really admit a suspicion into his heart of hearts.

Yet it was most strange that the thrust of a splinter into

his hand brought a cry from Thunder Moon, whereas even a three-year-old Cheyenne child would have scorned to utter so much as a whisper. And whereas the other children were already peeling off strips of skin from their arms and breasts as an offering to the gods of war, Thunder Moon could never be induced to submit to the knife.

"Let me show how easy it is, and how much it will please the Sky People!" said Big Hard Face, one day, and he deliberately ripped a strip of skin from his already scarred right arm.

His foster son covered his face.

"I shall help you!" said Big Hard Face.

But Thunder Moon screamed at the sight of the knife and wriggled away to find safety.

Big Hard Face was deeply distressed. He felt that this must be wrong, and yet in his heart of hearts there was that abiding faith in the boy.

The elders came to him, one day, and deliberately threw the shadow upon his mind, at the last.

For they said:

"We know, Big Hard Face, that the brave man sees all the world as brave. And the coward sees every man full of fear. And you, brother, cannot see well the thing that is nearest to you. You cannot look at your own chin. Neither can you look into your own heart. These things are hidden because of their nearness. So it is with your son. He is tall, and his shoulders are broad, and he rides horses worthy of the Sky People.

"But we have come to ask you to make sure that he is brave, Big Hard Face. Let him be tested. He is twelve years old. The other boys of such an age shoot arrows into trees and in play scalp even the stones. But Thunder Moon sits by himself and will not play with them. He will not ride a wild horse. And when he is wrestled down to the ground, he sits and weeps like a girl. No, there are no Cheyenne girls who would weep so!"

And they added: "Brother, be warned!"

How fatuous was Big Hard Face!

He pointed upward, and he merely said: "Do you judge the Sky People as though they were Cheyennes? Wait, wait! The hard winter brings the warmest spring!"

Chapter Four

"Big trees grow slowly," said Big Hard Face.

Thunder Moon remembered that saying. He took it into his heart and pondered much on it, and it was a comfort to him beyond all knowing. Sometimes, when he thought of his shortcomings, and of the misery and the shame in which he spent his days, he wished that it might all end suddenly in death, but when he looked to the ugly face of his foster father and considered the deathless faith which the warrior had in him, it revived his own courage a little. And he hoped that one day he would turn a corner and find himself a man, and worthy to be a Cheyenne.

He was thirteen, now.

And one day he laid aside the bow with which he had wandered out to practice at marks, and went down to the edge of the river in the heat of the morning to swim. On the verge, he paused. For here the stream had lost its current in a broad pool, and on the glassy surface he saw himself as in a great mirror. He had seen himself before, but never so clearly. And, as usual, he set about casting up the sum of the differences which existed between him and the other lads of the tribe. That matter of color—his sun-brown against their dark copper—was a small thing, for he had been weathered almost to their own hue, but there were other points of great dissimilarity. He was a little taller than the other boys of his age, but the distinctions did not lie in mere size.

His playmates, on the whole, were cast in one mold. Whether from riding, running, or swimming, their legs were well developed, lithe, and rounded. They were particularly large as compared with their arms; thousands of years of travel afoot had stamped these characteristics into the race. But the white man works with his hands and his arms, standing still at the carpenter's bench, or the blacksmith's forge, or bending in the furrow in the field.

Thunder Moon knew nothing about white men. No one had ever told him that he was of an alien race. But he could see that his legs were thinner, and his bones larger than those of the Cheyenne youngsters. His feet were smaller, his hips were narrower, his chest was deeper and his shoulders broader; there was a greater length and girth to his arms, and his hands were much bigger.

In the last year, he had begun to fill out; new blood was running in his veins, like spring sap in a young tree; new thoughts came to him. What had been very hard for him to understand the year before was now easy. He did not sleep so much, and waking was not such agony. His head was held straighter, there was more life in his step, and he could listen to the old men of the tribe without drowsing.

No other persons noticed the change, but Thunder Moon did. Because for many years, now, he had been acutely self-conscious. He was not like the others. He was slower and clumsier; he learned lessons with more difficulty; he forgot the command that was given to him the instant that he left the tepee, and in all things he could see that he was below the standard.

That he had other qualities of inward strength did not occur to him, and he would have been the first to agree with the others of the tribe, that the hours he spent in dreaming and thinking in solitude were worse than useless.

They had their use, but that usefulness would not appear at once. The metal that this boy was made of differed from that which composed the other youth of the Cheyennes. Through sundry millions of generations there had been gathered into him a different capacity. The great question was: Could such metal be shaped into the sort of tool which would cut according to the Cheyenne pattern?

Now, regarding himself with his usual critical mind—a

mind which had creased his young forehead with wrinkles which appeared on the brow of no youthful redskin of the nation—he shook his head once more.

Oh, for more suppleness! Oh, for lighter bones and greater grace!

He stood on a stone, gripping it with his toes, and prepared to make the dive as smooth and silent as possible. Oh, he knew lads of the tribe who could fling themselves from the highest bank, and yet disappear into the water with hardly a sound, while a long ripple rose and closed over the spot where their feet had disappeared. Marvels of grace they were, and as they flew through the air on their way to the surface of the pool, they seemed to be masters of the lightest element, also, like veritable birds.

Before he made his effort, he knew that he would fail. He knew exactly how it should be done. With the keen scrutiny of the backward man, he had studied in detail just how the best divers managed themselves. But he felt that he would never be able to apply the lessons which he had pored over.

Then, gritting his teeth, he sprang out and forward and down.

It was not a bad dive, as dives go, but as he struck the water, the force of it against his head, his breast, and all his body, told him that he had indeed failed ignominiously again.

Why, even the five-year-old girls of the tribe could dive far better than this!

He forced himself forward and down, swimming with long strokes, forcing himself ahead with a blind grimness. For whatever his weaknesses might be in other directions, at least, there was a reservoir of wind capacity in that deep chest of his. And he punished himself in this manner, until his reaching hands touched the bottom, the slimy, deep, soft mud.

At that, something stabbed him in the arm. He caught at the wounded place with his left hand, and that hand closed over something cold as the water itself, and slimy as the mud, and wriggling.

A beat of the other hand and a thrust of his feet against

the bottom carried him to the surface, and as he reached it, he saw his right hand had gripped a big water snake just below the head!

Its eyes glittered terribly at Thunder Moon, and its lithe body lashed the surface of the little lake into foam.

There were two kinds of those snakes, as Thunder Moon had heard. From the touch of one of them, strong men sickened and died. The bite of the other was less dangerous than the bite of a dog.

But which kind had stung him and was now held by him, he could not dream. His terror paralyzed him; actually greater than his dread of the snake was his fear lest terror itself should force him to release the viper and let it sting him again.

He struck out for the shore, swimming with all his might with the snake thrust out before him at the end of a stiffened arm. Across his face the horrible, whiplike body of the snake slashed. It curled around the arm which held it, but still Thunder Moon did not let go.

And if he could master the creature with the might of his hands, would he not master the poison which might be in it, also?

He stood dripping on the shore, at last. Then he was amazed at the prodigious length and thickness of the creature. If he had grasped it in any other place, he could not have spanned its body. Only here behind the head, the neck was shaped small and fitted his hand. But yes, how huge it was, and still he held it safely, thrust far from his body, and it yawned its vast, ugly mouth in vain, and it thrust its tongue in and out, and displayed the curved and ominous fangs with which it was armed.

Suddenly it came to Thunder Moon that this was an exploit of which even one of the braves might be proud; far more, one of the young men of the tribe. And he, a boy, had done it! He had heard his father say that there was a great grip in his hand, and now here was the proof of it!

He smashed the head of the serpent on a rock and then measured it, with the greatest care, in length and circumference. Better still to take home the skin as a proof.

He paused, for he felt that after all they would not believe what he said, even though he should be able to show them the punctures in his wrist—unless those punctures showed the poison soon!

He looked at them curiously. There was a little run of blood from each of them, but otherwise they were of no importance. There was very little pain. And he felt another pang of wonder.

How was it that he was not sitting cross-legged on the bank, rocking himself to and fro, and howling with fear?

Thunder Moon blushed more deeply than any true Indian could have done. He had been ashamed before, but never like this. For now it was as though he had been suddenly divided from himself. On the one hand was the weak creature which had stumbled through life, worsted by every circumstance. On the other hand there was a brand-new self which had been bitten in the depths of the lake and had grappled with a great snake and carried it safely to the shore and destroyed it.

His eye fell to the serpent and measured it again from the tip of the head to the slenderly fashioned tip of the tail. Truly, it was a comforting thought to him!

But, in the meantime, there was another peril before him. Had not someone told him, that where there was one snake there was sure to be a second? The male and the female lived in pairs, and if one were killed the second would come to seek revenge!

He even thought that he saw a slender shadow glance through the water, and the glimmer of a pair of eyes watching him and waiting for him, when he should swim back to regain the bank on which he had left his bow.

He stepped back suddenly to the edge of the water.

"I have discovered a new self with no fear in me!" said Thunder Moon. "It is the gift of the Sky People!"

He caught up the limp, dead body of the snake and raised it to the heavens.

"I offer it to you in token of my thanks, Sky People," said Thunder Moon. "My knife shall not touch it. I shall not boast of it to the men of the tribe. I shall not even tell

my father. Because it is my gift to you, and you and I
alone shall know about it!"

Now when he had said that, the last shadow of fear left
him. He looked with a calm eye upon the waters before
him, and he knew that the Sky People had indeed looked
down upon him and heard his voice!

Chapter Five

As a matter of fact, he was acting very much as an Indian boy might have acted under the same circumstances,
except that there was in Thunder Moon a sensitiveness of
soul such as few Indian boys ever possessed. He opened
his heart at a stroke, and a vast confidence in his destiny
flowed in upon him.

Then he dived from the shore, hardly thinking of what
he did, but behold! The water curled around his toes with
hardly a ripple, and he felt his body gliding smoothly
through the lake. Joy flamed into the soul of Thunder
Moon; this was no little thing to him; there was no one to
tell him that we often do things better when we relax
confidently; to him this was an open and manifest proof
that the spirits which rule man had entered him and were
giving him strength and skill.

He skimmed up to the surface again. The danger of a
second snake in these waters was not even in his mind.
He was occupied with his swimming, and certainly he had
never swum so joyously and well. He reached the bank.
He leaped up to his full height, brown body flashing in the
sun, and his war whoop rang across the plain.

All things were suddenly possible.

He gripped the bow which he had left on the bank. He
drew it back to his very ear with no effo t. He sent the
blunt-headed arrow at the trunk of a tree, and the arrow
stood quivering and humming in the very center of that
target!

Thunder Moon was only thirteen. That should be remembered. And at that age a boy can put on a new self like a new suit of clothes. That was exactly what he did. Not new in all respects, but new in certain ones.

For instance, he had always feared the company of his peers, but now he wanted to be seen and known by the other boys of the tribe. He wanted them to see what he could do. Above all, let Big Hard Face know that his faith had been justified!

He jogged down the bank of the stream, therefore, toward the place where he knew the other children were swimming and where, later, they would be running and wrestling on the bank. He stood upon a little hill, at last, and listened to the piping of their voices and saw the swirl of their games, and listened to the splashings of the water.

Then he walked lightly down to meet them.

They should have seen even from a distance that this was a different lad from the one they had always mocked and scorned, but the eyes of boyhood are blind, blind eyes. Now they regarded him with shrugged shoulders and with open laughter.

"Thunder Moon!"

It was a voice of command, and it came from Waiting Bear. He really should not have been playing among the boys, because, though he was only fifteen, he had already ridden in a war party, and he had counted *coup* upon the body of a dead Pawnee. He was a warrior, and a fit companion for the fighting men of the tribe. But he had come down here to the river bank to sun himself in the admiration of his former friends.

"Thunder Moon!" said Waiting Bear. "Give me your bow. I am going to shoot that hawk. It thinks that there are only children here, but I am going to show it that there is a brave among them!"

In fact, the hawk was floating very low in the air, with a lazy insolence. Sometimes it rested in the top of a small cottonwood on the bank of the stream, and sometimes it drifted out again in a low circle. It must have been an old and wise bird, knowing the difference between the powers of children and the powers of men. Never would it have ventured so close to the war bows of the Cheyennes.

"Do you hear me, Thunder Moon?"

"I hear you, Waiting Bear. But my bow is too strong for you to draw. You could not use it!"

In an instant, as though a danger signal had been given, all the noise of the playing ceased, and there was a broad silence lying upon the river and the banks of it. Every head turned toward the two—to Thunder Moon in amazement, and toward Waiting Bear in fearful expectation.

For when a brave has been defied by a child, he must punish the latter.

Waiting Bear, however, could hardly believe his ears. Not a week before, he had cuffed this Thunder Moon upon the ear and sent him howling home to his father's tepee.

So he called again: "Are you mad, Thunder Moon?"

"Take a little play bow, Waiting Bear," said this strange new foster son of Big Hard Face. "Do not strain your arms uselessly with the big war bows. But I shall show you how this bow should be used!"

He put an arrow on the string and watched the hawk sailing out from the cottonwood on broad pinions.

"Sky People," said Thunder Moon in his heart of hearts, "let them all know what strength you have given me!"

There was a little cloud floating in the center of the heavens, filled with snowy brilliance beyond the brilliance of pearls. And somehow the sight of it gave a greater assurance to Thunder Moon. Just over his head the hawk swept, and raising his bow suddenly, he pulled the shaft far back and let drive.

He made sure that it would pass harmlessly, far in front of the bird above him. But the soft flight of the sailing hawk was incredibly fast. Straight into the line of the danger it sped, then saw the slender, flying shadow and veered with a great beat of the wings.

It was too late. The arrow drove home, a tuft of feathers fluttered down. They heard the angry, terrified scream of the bird of prey which strove to wing away. But those broad pinions were half nerveless already. It staggered in the air, it descended in a ragged circle, then lost balance and tumbled over and over in the air and landed on its back with an audible thud at the very feet of Thunder Moon.

Waiting Bear, who had begun to make an angry approach toward the other, halted in astonishment, and a tingling shout of wonder rang from all the boys. They instantly hushed themselves. He who had performed that great feat was about to speak, and suddenly he had become one worth listening to.

He said in a voice which he forced into matter-of-factness: "You saw the hawk dodge, but my arrow turned also in the air and followed it. I had told it to go straight to the heart of that hawk, and you see that it was afraid to disobey me. This is something that you should learn also, Waiting Bear."

He stopped and drew the arrow out and raised its red tip silently to the blue heavens above him. He did not speak aloud, but in his heart of hearts he said fervently: "For this, much thanks!"

Then he turned his back on the fallen hawk and went and sat down a little apart from the rest on the fallen trunk of a tree. He was trembling with joy and with pride so that he could not trust himself to mix with his fellows at once. And they, drawing together in knots, whispered and nodded eagerly for a moment. Then some of them went and drew out the best feathers of the bird which Thunder Moon had treated with such contempt, and they cut off its wings.

He did not apparently regard them, and yet in his heart he was glad, because he knew that when those wings were carried back into the camp, men would ask questions, and the story would be told, and then they would know of the thing which he had done. But as for himself, he had vowed a second time that he would not boast.

"People of the Sky," said Thunder Moon in his heart of hearts as he sat by the river, "I am nothing. It is what you have poured into me that counts. This morning I was only a stupid and stumbling boy. I was an empty basket, but you chose to pour me full of treasures of strength and courage. Now I am strong, and I am not afraid!"

He looked back across the assemblage of the other boys who were returning to their games, and above their heads he encountered the angry glance of Waiting Bear. However, he knew that the latter would not take any direct notice of the insult which had been so openly offered to him. Later on, as time offered, Waiting Bear would strive to take the chance which might humiliate his rival.

But there was something more than anger in the glance of Waiting Bear. There was wonder, and awe, also. The old bull looks with amazement at the half-grown steer which dares to offer him battle!

"Thunder Moon! Thunder Moon!" came a sharp cry of many voices. "Enter the race. You run well!"

And they shrieked with laughter. Thunder Moon's heart sank in him. He looked up to the blue sky, but small comfort flowed back upon his soul. To run a half mile out and a half mile back, which was the usual distance for a trial of speed, was, he felt, perfectly hopeless. He could not match himself against the lithe, lightly poised bodies of the other Cheyennes.

And yet over another and a shorter course he might win, perhaps—if the Sky People would blow him forward with their helping breath.

The voice of Waiting Bear: "Are you afraid to stand up and run? Are you afraid that I will beat you too badly, Thunder Moon?"

This was a form of challenge which he could not very well refuse. He stood up, but his heart was filled with doubt. Too often he had matched himself against even the little youngsters on the sandy banks of the river, and though he might fly away ahead of all, at first, in the end his legs grew leaden, and his chest was filled with fire, and they all brushed past him before the finish. Much he feared for the result now!

However, he could not refuse the test. He walked very

slowly down toward them, gathering his dignity about him like a robe.

"Look yonder, Waiting Bear." He pointed to a lightning-blasted willow, white as a ghost, and naked as a pole. It was a hundred paces off. "Look yonder. I shall run against you to that tree and back. Only to show you that it is easy for me to beat you. I do not care to waste my time running a long race."

Chapter Six

The teeth of Waiting Bear flashed in the intensity of his rage.

"You talk in a very loud voice," said he. "I hear you, and I laugh. Perhaps the people in the tepees will hear you, also. But they will only smile. They are tired of laughing at Thunder Moon. However, do you really mean that you will run against me—against Waiting Bear?"

"Do you think that is wonderful?" said Thunder Moon, rejoicing inwardly. For he could see that his taunts had made the other tremble with rage and moisture had started out on his forehead. After all, it was easy to taunt, and if the Sky People chose to give him speed thereafter, it was well. But if they did not choose, at least he would have had the glory of making the new warrior, Waiting Bear, act like a peevish woman. All the eyes of the others were upon them. And the eyes of those boys would not fail to see everything. Their sympathy was already upon the side of Thunder Moon, for through many days, now, they had been suffering under the tyranny of their old playmate, Waiting Bear.

With all their hearts they wished that he might be beaten, but with all their hearts they disbelieved that he could be, for his flying feet had knocked up sand into all their faces, at one time or another.

"I think it is not wonderful, but very foolish," said

Waiting Bear. "And I should not care to run against a fool for nothing."

"Do you wish to bet?" asked Thunder Moon seriously —for a contest on which there was betting was a serious matter indeed. It became almost as important as a feat in war.

He glanced upward. It seemed to him that the small white cloud had doubled in size and in brilliancy, and strength and assurance flowed in upon the heart of the boy suddenly.

"I will bet you the price of one of those long-legged horses which your father has given to you."

Thunder Moon bit his lip. Of all things on earth, those horses were most dear to him. Of all things on earth, those chestnut steeds with the dashes of white on the forehead were most valued by his father, also.

"If you were to search your tepee," said Thunder Moon calmly, "what could you find worth the price of one of my horses?"

Waiting Bear stamped in a rage. It was true that his father was not as wealthy as Thunder Moon. And he himself had not yet accumulated any riches except— He gasped and his eyes distended and his voice almost choked as he cried: "I have two running horses, and—"

"Two running horses?" Thunder Moon smiled. "Why should I want them, when my own horses can carry me twice as fast as two of yours?"

"And I have a rifle in my tepee that never fails of its mark!" shouted Waiting Bear.

The whole nation knew about that rifle. For the father of Waiting Bear, mad with joy because his boy had accomplished a *coup* on a Pawnee at this early age, had bought for him one of the finest and newest of rifles. It was long-barreled, and yet it was light as a plaything, and it shot harder and farther than any other gun among the Cheyennes. Even such a boy as Waiting Bear became formidable with such a weapon in his hands.

Thunder Moon listened, and his heart beat with such a violence that it seemed to be tearing through his breast.

"Two horses and that gun—against one horse of mine?"

"Against only one, the tall one, with the white stockings on both forefeet."

He had put his finger exactly upon the sore spot. It was the prize of all the herd. It was a very eagle for speed and endurance, and Thunder Moon winced in spite of himself. However, he felt that he had committed himself too far to draw back, and as for bargaining, it was like an insult to the Sky People. Only through their strength could he win, he felt sure, and if their strength was loaned to him, why need he fear to wager all the horses against the value of a feather?

"I shall accept that bet," said he.

Waiting Bear leaped into the air and struck his hands together above him, while his yell smote the face of the swimming pool and echoed sharply back to him.

"It is mine! The great horse is mine!" he screeched. "You are all witnesses of what he has promised!"

"We are witnesses," the others admitted.

Then they looked with a sort of gloomy wonder at Thunder Moon, as though amazed that even such a stupid fellow as he should have risked such a dreadful loss! For to be mounted upon the back of that silver-footed marvel was to be on the back of a great bird. It was to be beyond pursuit, and it was to be able to overtake with ease every living thing that roamed upon the prairie. Even the winged antelope would have to surrender to such a hunter!

No wonder, therefore, that they stared in pity and in contempt, and in wonder at Thunder Moon.

But for his part, he had shut his mind resolutely against the possibility of loss.

He looked askance at the radiant face of his rival, as they stood on the mark.

"However, Waiting Bear, I shall let you shoot the gun, once in a long time!"

Waiting Bear started, and scowled bitterly at his companion.

"You have very little sense, Thunder Moon," said he.

"However, I shall beat you so far that before I finish, I shall stop to pick up some sand and throw it in your face!"

But Thunder Moon merely laughed. He had a feeling that the nervous rage of his rival might not lend any speed to his feet. And he said in addition:

"Remember, Waiting Bear. The hawk also thought that I was only a boy. And the hawk is dead!"

Waiting Bear stamped in impotent rage, and then with his teeth set and his lips strained back from them he waved to the starter to give the signal.

"Now, People of the Sky," said Thunder Moon in his heart, looking upward, "make my wits light and quick. Make my eyes see the best place to step. Give wings to my feet. You have killed the hawk and the snake with my hands. And all the honor that you give to me, I give back to you."

The starter had stretched out his arms, ready to strike his hands together, which was the starting signal. Waiting Bear leaned far forward, tense with preparedness.

"Wait a moment," said Thunder Moon. "I am not yet ready."

The starter relaxed.

"Are we to stand here all day?" exclaimed Waiting Bear.

He was in a fury, and Thunder Moon merely laughed. He could guess that all of this rage would blind his rival, and blind men do not run well.

For his own part, he was marking the course with a keen eye. The Sky People had made him calm in spite of the great wager for which he was running; and that meant that they intended him to use his wits. Use them he would, and he saw that the straight line to the tree was through soft sand, but a little to the right, the waters of the river had risen during the flood time of the spring, and there the ground surface was more compacted and firm. It would not slide back half so much beneath his gripping toes.

In the meantime, he rubbed off the bottom of his feet. He stretched his legs, one at a time, leisurely, and he smiled around him at the tense faces of the spectators, and at Waiting Bear.

"You are all witnesses," said he, "that Waiting Bear wanted to make the wager. I did not wish to steal the rifle from him!"

There was a snort of fury from Waiting Bear.

"Ready!" called Thunder Moon sharply.

The starter smote his hands together, and off they leaped. But Waiting Bear, for all his tenseness, was last off the mark, and thus gave his enemy a vital stride of advantage.

There was a yell of wonder from the onlookers, for they saw the younger contestant swerve suddenly to the right, and thus abandon his advantage.

Waiting Bear, seeing this swerve, could not help giving a glance to the side, and an excited yelp of triumph, while he drove straightforward toward the mark. But, in the meantime, Thunder Moon had the firmer ground beneath his feet. There was no backward slipping. And as he ran, it seemed to him that his feet had turned wonderfully light, and that his stride was stretched out and lengthened miraculously.

He gained on his rival, he passed him, and well in the lead he touched the blasted tree and whirled about.

He saw an expression of frozen terror and incredulity on the face of Waiting Bear—the very look of the beaten man who cannot understand how his defeat has been accomplished. And back went Thunder Moon, veering sharply to the left, this time, to regain the best footing.

Behind him came the stretching shadow of his rival. The black head and shoulders of the young brave drifted across the sands beside Thunder Moon, gaining fast. But the race was short. Yonder was the line. The screaming voices of the spectators tore the ears of Thunder Moon. He set his teeth and sprang forward with a last effort at the same moment that he was conscious of Waiting Bear rushing up beside him on even terms.

And then they were past the line.

He turned back, dizzy and half blinded, and as he did so, he saw them all running toward him, and Waiting

Bear, his head hanging, was walking slowly back toward
the distant tepees, whose pointed tops showed against the
sky line.

He had won!

The boys surrounded him with shrill clamor, slapping
him, praising his speed, his courage, his cleverness, envy-
ing him the matchless rifle which was to be his.

But Thunder Moon, gasping for breath and smiling,
looked up to the blue of the sky, and to the shining white
cloud which drifted across its face.

As he looked, it dissolved swiftly. The Sky People had
performed their work!

Chapter Seven

It was more or less a triumphal procession that
Thunder Moon led back to the village to the lodge of the
father of Waiting Bear. He stood before the tepee and
saw Waiting Bear, with a face set like iron, bear forth the
great prize, a shining rifle, light, trim, beautifully bal-
anced. Not half the warriors in the tribe possessed
firearms, and not a single man had anything to show that
was comparable with this.

Thunder Moon carried that trophy back to the lodge of
Big Hard Face and found he had just returned from
hunting, with his horse loaded down with buffalo meat.
He forgot the results of his hunting trip, however, when
he saw his foster child with the rifle in his hands, surrounded by this little herd of admiring youngsters.

Big Hard Face took the boy and the gun together and
lifted them triumphantly above his head toward the sky,
and he gave thanks with all his heart.

And he cried aloud: "You thought that his heart was
dead. But it was only sleeping. And there has never before been such a man among the Cheyennes. You shall
see hereafter!"

And then he took the lad to the interior of the tepee and sat him down, shutting out all saving White Crow. She was busy with her evening cookery, and even her hard and withered face lighted with interest as she watched and listened.

"Now," said Big Hard Face, taking the rifle with a covetous touch, "tell me everything that has happened, and I shall see that this gun never lacks food, and you shall practice with it until your hand is steadier than a rock and the eagle falls out of the sky when you fire!"

Thunder Moon smiled. His whole heart was loosened and dissolved and ready to pour itself out in talk, but he restrained himself with a mighty effort, for he remembered the compact that he had made with the Sky People. They had fulfilled their part of the bargain, and they had given him glory enough. For his part, he was not to boast.

He sighed. He had not dreamed that it would be so fearfully difficult to keep his self-esteem under control.

"It was nothing," said Thunder Moon. "It was only that Waiting Bear and I ran a race for a bet. The big stallion, against this gun and two of his horses. He will send the horses to your tepee later!"

And suddenly he jumped up and bolted from the lodge, but as he went out he heard the voice of his foster father exclaiming, half stifled with pride:

"Do you hear, White Crow? He is also modest! He will not boast!"

"Tush!" said that evil-minded old dame. "You will find that at bottom there is something of which he has to be ashamed!"

In the meantime, Waiting Bear had poured out his story in a passion of grief to his father. The latter listened with a stony face, but his eyes were fire; the possession of that gun had been their greatest family treasure.

"Big medicine has been working for young Thunder Moon," said he at the end. "Tell me if there was nothing strange when you ran?"

"Yes, yes!" answered Waiting Bear passionately. "My feet were as heavy as two stones, and something breathed against me and pushed me back!"

His father nodded.

"We shall take the back trail of Thunder Moon," said he, "and find out what medicine he made, if we can. I have seen you both run, and he can no more beat you in a fair race than a crow can beat a hawk!"

Accordingly, they picked up the back trail of Thunder Moon on the bank of the river and followed it with scrupulous care until they came to the little lake across which he had swum, and on the farther side, they found the great dead snake, its head smashed in, and trains of ants already making procession toward it. There was no doubt about the identity of him who had killed it. The chief lifted the long, heavy body and held it at arm's length.

"Look!" said he. "What medicine gave him the power to beat you in the race, to shoot the hawk out of the sky, and the courage to taunt you to your face? It was the medicine of the snake, which he caught in the bottom of the river and carried to the land and killed. Could he have swum down and back with such a weight, except for his medicine that was helping him? Therefore, do not be ashamed. He has a big medicine; it is the medicine that beat you, and not Thunder Moon!"

They went back to the village, and instantly the tale was repeated, and it was everywhere believed, because this awakening of Thunder Moon was almost the strangest thing that had ever happened in the Cheyenne tribe. Incidentally, affairs were magnified a good deal. It was only natural that the size of the snake should be multiplied by two or three, and that the height at which the hawk had been flying should be doubled, and that the ease with which Thunder Moon had beaten Waiting Bear in the race should be turned into a prodigious thing, so that it was accepted that a miracle had been wrought for Thunder Moon on this day.

Such was the manner in which the story was made known, and the more perfectly Thunder Moon kept his silence about the subject, the more it was romanced about, until it had become a thing of epic proportions.

Thunder Moon was himself more than a little frightened by the disturbance this had caused. Now that he looked back upon the day, he could hardly tell whether it had been a dream or not, and something told him that the Sky People, who had so manifestly befriended him, would never do so again.

However, he bent himself desperately to a great effort, in order that he might afterward be able to prove himself at least as good as the other boys of the tribe. He knew that he was slow and clumsy of foot, and that his running powers sufficed only for a short sprint, and that he was awkward with knife or bow and arrows, and that he could not scorn pain as the other youngsters did, and that he was far from being their equal in sharpness of eye. But at least a magnificent weapon had been confided to his hands. Should he not make the most of that? That, and the fleet horses which his father owned?

He had Big Hard Face show him all about the care of a rifle. And that delighted Indian gave an ample supply of precious ammunition into his hands. After that, from dawn to dark, the gun was never out of his hands.

It had become a religion to Thunder Moon. Having failed at all else, he dared not fail at this. He lay awake at night, pondering his faults of the day and the manner of correcting them. He awakened from his sleep with sudden twitchings and jerkings, and found himself in the middle of a great dream in which the rifle was achieving monstrous things. The crease between his eyes was sunk deeper than ever, but at the same time, those eyes grew brighter and steadier. The dullness of continual bafflement began to leave them, and a grim resolution took its place. Big Hard Face, all of these days, watched the progress of his son with an intense anxiety and joy. He could hardly believe that his hopes were in process of being fulfilled. And yet here were the indubitable signs of it.

There was only one poison in his life, and that was supplied by his withered aunt, White Crow, whose croaking voice never dwelt upon anything except the deficiencies of Thunder Moon.

"You will see how it is in the end," she said. "Now he lies and speaks like a man. But he is still a coward, and he will always be a coward! I saw him yesterday knock his shin against your bow, and his face wrinkled up like the face of a baby about to cry."

"Look!" said Big Hard Face sullenly and savagely. "All the goodness and the kindness has been taken from you. There was once enough of it in you to make you smooth. Now it is gone and you are full of wrinkles and emptiness! I tell you, Thunder Moon will be a great chief!"

"You yourself are afraid to test him!" she cried.

"Afraid? White Crow, I do not wish to say that you lie, but I fear that I shall have to."

"Do I lie?" she answered. "Then I shall tell you a way to know whether or not he is a coward."

"What way?" he asked. "Would you have him fight a bear hand to hand?"

"Not that. But a little thing. Every good Cheyenne boy is not afraid to do it when he comes close to manhood."

"Very well, tell me."

"What do the boys do in honor of Tarawa, and to give themselves good luck on the warpath? They have their breasts pierced, and thongs passed through them, and they try to tear the thongs through the flesh."

Big Hard Face started to answer, and then, remembering the horror with which his son looked upon pain, he checked himself. He wished with all his heart that this subject had never been brought up.

"Tomorrow," said White Crow, "Waiting Bear will have his breasts slashed, and the thong will be passed through the cuts. Now, nephew, if you have faith in your son, place him on the hill by the side of Waiting Bear. Let us see your son bear pain!"

Big Hard Face rubbed his knuckles across his forehead, and then he shouted hoarsely: "I shall do it! I shall do it, White Crow! Go tell all the old women! They may go tomorrow and watch, and they will see what a man Thunder Moon has become!"

Chapter Eight

"Tarawa, who rules in the top of the sky and the bottom of the earth, and who made everything and watches over everything—Tarawa," said Big Hard Face, "loves the Cheyennes more than all the other peoples of the earth; more than he loves the Dakotas, or the Pawnees, or the Osages, or the Comanches, or the whites."

Here he paused a little and looked fixedly at the boy; but the eyes of Thunder Moon did not waver. It was plain that, as yet, he did not suspect that his blood was really different from that of the tribe. There had been a sort of unvoiced understanding through the tribe that the real parentage of Thunder Moon should never be discussed in his hearing.

No, the eyes of the boy were fixed upon the face of his foster father merely with a deep interest. Of late, he had adopted this manner whenever his elders spoke about the Sky People; as though he weighed these matters in his mind. Therefore, all of the Cheyennes felt that this boy knew some big medicine. They were the more sure of it because he never spoke of the matter.

"Tarawa," went on the father, "loves the Cheyennes, but he wishes to make sure that the Cheyennes are worthy of him. And when he looks down at a party on the warpath, how is Tarawa to know the good Cheyennes from the bad ones?"

He made another pause.

Thunder Moon frowned, but he could not penetrate to the hidden meaning.

"I can't tell," said he.

And Big Hard Face, looking down again at the arrow

40

which his hands were almost automatically shaping and smoothing, said in continuation:

"He must have some sign. The eyes of Tarawa can see everything, but they must see a sign so that he can distinguish man from man. Look! There is Lame Eagle!"

Both Big Hard Face and his son forgot all else for the moment and fixed their attention upon the great war leader of the tribe, who was at that moment passing in the company of the great medicine man, White Rain. The latter, as usual, had his head bowed, and his scowling glance fixed upon the earth, as though he were reading a trail; but Lame Eagle's face was ever lifted, and the wind stirred the magnificent feathers that rose straight above his head and drooped down his back. He greeted them with a pleasant word.

"May your days be long, and may buffalo meat be ever in your lodge, Big Hard Face!"

Then he passed on, touching the ground lightly with his staff; and, as he went by, the sun made the bright bead work arabesques on his deerskin suit gleam.

Gentle in speech, slow in counsel, a thunderbolt in war, it had been long since that tribe of the Cheyennes had possessed such a leader; and the eyes of both the boy and his foster father glistened as they watched the great man out of sight.

"But even the face of Lame Eagle," went on the older man, turning back to his theme, "cannot always be known to Tarawa. For there is a hurrying and sweeping of men, in the battle. But first, he sees the feathers of the chief, then he looks more closely. He sees that the arms of Lame Eagle are covered with scars where he has torn away the skin in honor of the gods. And he looks more closely still; and he sees a great, ragged white scar over each breast. Then he knows that this is a brave man, who loves the Sky People; and Tarawa puts strength into the hand of Lame Eagle."

"It may be so," said Thunder Moon slowly.

His foster father's face darkened.

"It is always thus!" said he impatiently. "When the other young men of the Cheyennes sit with their elders,

they write down in their minds the words which they hear
and strive only to remember them; but Thunder Moon
first thinks and tries to judge for himself. Is he a man to
judge and think? Has he killed so much as a buffalo calf
in all his life?"

Tears brimmed the eyes of the boy, and his foster father, more disturbed than ever, glanced hastily away.
There was so much woman in this boy, that half the time
his heart failed him; and he was filled with doubts about
the future of the lad.

He looked back at the broad shoulders, and the arched
chest, and the mighty muscles which were beginning to
form along the arms. No other lad in the tribe could boast
of such a torso. The confidence of Big Hard Face began
to return.

"However, hear what I have to say, and then you will
see that I am right. When Tarawa looks down on the
band which steals along the warpath, he first marks down
the brave men, who carry the signs of their bravery with
them. Then he gives them power and fortune.

"But you, when you ride on the warpath—what signs
do you bear? Have you the feathers of a chief in your
hair? Are you marked with the scars of battle or of self-
torture in which you have honored Tarawa?"

The face of Thunder Moon grew blank.

"Now," went on his father, "this very day, on the eastern hill toward the sun, young Waiting Bear is to have his
breasts opened with the knife and the thongs passed
through them. You and I shall go up with him. I shall cut
your breasts with the knife. I shall pass the thong through
the cuts. There will be a little blood and a little pain. But
afterward, when you come back to my tepee, the mark of
your manhood will be upon your body for the whole tribe
to know that you are worthy to be a brave, and Tarawa
will be ready to welcome another warrior!"

He stood up and extended his hand, and Thunder
Moon's eyes widened, and his face turned pale.

"Come!" said the foster father. "We shall go at once!"

He stood up and extended his hand, and Thunder
Moon seemed to need its assistance as he got to his feet.

Side by side, they went out from the village; but as they went, the voice of Big Hard Face was continually raised.

"Look!" he would cry. "Here walks Thunder Moon ready to climb up to the eastern hill and be tied, through his body, to the post of sacrifice. Here walks Thunder Moon, ready to be seen by the Sky People. Look well at him, oh, ye Cheyennes! This is a warrior! This is the true son of Big Hard Face."

The cry caused a continual commotion, and children and women and men poured out to see the pair pass.

Thunder Moon, seeing the wonder in their faces, as though this were the very last thing that they could have expected from him, felt his courage expand. He smiled. He put back his head. His step grew lighter. And he told himself that he would die sooner than fail in this great test.

And, as they left the village and began the ascent, they saw Waiting Bear and his grandfather already before them on the high place. Many people stood at a distance, to watch what was to happen.

"Half of your life is spent with honor, when you do this thing," said Big Hard Face. "All the tribe will honor you. Men, and even the children, used to smile at you before you took the rifle from Waiting Bear. But now you have a chance to do a greater thing by showing them all, that, while Waiting Bear may endure the torment with silence, you may endure it with a smile. But if Waiting Bear should fail in the trial, do you know what would happen to him?"

The boy half closed his eyes and shuddered. He knew only too well.

Two years before, one of the youths of the tribe had shrunk from the knife and begged for mercy. Instantly, he had been released from the danger. He had been sent freely back to the village. But from that moment he began to live as one who had died while he still breathes, and walks, and speaks. The men of the tribe would not sit in the same lodge with him. When he entered a tepee, even some of the women and children scorned to breathe the atmosphere which his presence polluted. And, indeed, he had ceased to be a man. He had become a woman, with a single, shambling rackbones of a horse assigned to him; and instead of the glories of the warpath, he was given the woman's work of fleshing the buffalo robes.

Of him, Thunder Moon thought; and his heart was sick in him. The very children of the village turned their backs upon the disgraced youth. Death, certainly, was preferable to such an existence. And, for his own part, he was determined to die rather than fail.

So he climbed up the hill, pale, but with his jaw resolutely set.

And at the top he saw Waiting Bear standing boldly. A leather thong was already knotted in his flesh. Now, the old Indian who had accompanied Waiting Bear slashed the other side twice and fastened the other thong in place.

Then, leaning back his weight against the two leather strips, which were attached to the post in the center, Waiting Bear walked slowly, his grandfather aiding in pushing against him, so as to throw a strain upon the tied flesh. It seemed that it must give and that the thongs would tear through and set him free. But the skin held. The sinews were tough, and the agony would have to continue until the night.

All the blood seemed to have left the brain of Thunder Moon and he leaned heavily against his foster father.

"Do you hear me?" said Big Hard Face roughly.

"I hear you!" whispered the boy.

"What is one day of pain compared with a long life of glory? Thunder Moon, is your heart stronger?"

"Give me a little moment longer. The sun has made me dizzy!"

There was a faint groan from the warrior.

"They are watching. We cannot wait any longer!" he cautioned, and at the same time he gripped the flesh over the right breast of Thunder Moon and drew it stiffly out from his body. The knife was raised and flashed. The brightness of it burned into the very soul of Thunder

Moon. Then a pang of exquisite agony pierced his body
—to the very heart, it seemed to him.

His strength melted from him. His throat muscles unlocked. And a scream of terror burst from his lips!

Chapter Nine

For a thing so dreadful, there was only one answer,
and that was terrible silence. A stifled moan from Big
Hard Face, as he knelt beside the fallen body of the boy,
was the only sound.

The grandfather of Waiting Bear had thrown his buffalo robe over his face, so that he might not see this shame-
ful spectacle. And all the distant watchers were frozen in
their places.

Then said Waiting Bear:

"Is not this a holy hill, which Tarawa is watching? Who
has brought a dog here, to howl at the sky?"

And he laughed, savagely, and throwing his weight back
more vigorously than ever, he seemed as though he would
straightway tear the leather thongs through his flesh. So
did he rejoice in his strength and in his scorn for pain.

But Thunder Moon crawled to his knees, and then to
his feet, staggering. He reached out a hand toward Big
Hard Face, but the latter was already striding on in advance, and his head, also, was veiled in his robe.

Then Thunder Moon grew aware of the brightness of the
terrible sun above him. And he saw in the heart of the sky
a little glistening cloud of white, already fast dissolving.

Why had he not known that the Sky People would not
fail him; that they had come down to watch; that they
would have given him succor if he had thought to call
upon them, and would have poured him full of strength?

But he had forgotten, and now he was worse than a
dead thing; he was a man-woman, the rest of his days!
He could not ride a war horse. He could not take a war

bow in his hands. The splendid rifle was no longer for him!

And now, worst of all, he must walk back into the village under the eyes of all these people.

He could not endure it. He turned and fled straight out across the sun-whitened prairies.

He ran until his head reeled and the ground waved beneath him. And when he looked back, the village had sunk from sight beneath the low swells of the prairie lands.

Then he sat down.

He took out his hunting knife. But the very sight of it was too much for him, and he knew, with a fresh and dreadful burst of shame, that he would not have the courage to strike himself to the heart.

So he flung himself downward and began to weep.

Perhaps in all the history of the Cheyenne tribe, no boy of thirteen had wept in such a fashion. He had been raised a Cheyenne, but what a hopeless distance lay between him and the fulfillment of the Indian ideal!

Afterward, with the heat of the sun scorching him, he sat up and looked toward the sky, and saw a crystal cloud of white, sailing up from the horizon.

He watched it in utter fascination, for it never entered his head that it had been sent other than a special sign from the Sky People to him.

He saw it drift higher and higher. It seemed to grow in size. It mounted to the very center of the sky, and there it hovered.

He could swear that it remained fixed in that place, and began to grow larger, and larger, and brighter and brighter, until the whole glory of the sun was bursting out from it, and covering the universe with a dazzling white radiance.

He threw his arms above his head, with the palms of his hands turned up.

"Tarawa! Tarawa! Tarawa!" he cried. "I am worse than a dog; I am weaker than a woman; I am meaner than a dead coyote. Kill me now with your own thunder. I do not wish to live if I cannot be a good Cheyenne!"

Yes; he could vow that the cloud sank lower toward him. He tensed himself, waiting for the leaping of the thunderbolt; but it did not come, the cloud did not divide. And then tears again burst from his eyes and blinded him.

They were tears of joy and relief; for it seemed to him that there could have been no surer token that Tarawa did indeed place some value upon his life, and that the Sky People still saw some value in him.

When he had recovered himself again, his melancholy was less frantic, more steady and subdued. He saw a little huddle of brush about a water hole; and there he went to drink, and to be in the shade, and to think.

What he should do, he could not guess until the dark of the evening came.

Then, with hunger beginning to torture him, he stood up and began to journey back toward the village.

In the near distance, he paused and listened to the voices which floated out from it. All was so near and dear to Thunder Moon that it seemed to him he could recognize the very voices of the dogs; and certainly he knew the hoarse howling of that gray beast which belonged to the lodge of the medicine man, White Rain.

I cannot tell you how it made the heart of the boy ache to recognize this sound, and to remember the dark, stern, mysterious face of the master of the dog, and all the friendly faces that thronged in upon his memory, and all of the well-known tepees, with their designs etched upon the buffalo skins. But when he thought of the horribly ugly face of poor Big Hard Face, then he burst into tears and wept his heart out.

Afterward, he stole forward. It was true that, in comparison to Indian boys, he was a clumsy craftsman upon the trail. Still, he knew things which probably no other white boy in the world was familiar with. He could read at a glance signs that would have been invisible to the eyes of most white men, and he knew how to slip through a field of the tall prairie grass in the summer without making a sound and hardly a ripple in the tops of the grasses. He could do all of these things, and you may be sure that now he seemed to melt into the darkness of the surface of the ground.

He passed the outpost which rode rounds and kept guard all the night through; for the great chief Lame Eagle maintained some semblance of military order among his people. He went on to the outermost circle of the lodges, and as he passed on hands and knees the very first of the lot, he heard talk on subjects near to his heart.

For there, by the tepee of Little Beaver, surrounded by that great warrior, his friends and his family, stood the tallest, the noblest, the swiftest of all that wonderful race of horses whose forbears had been brought back from the far land by Big Hard Face. They were discussing the points of the stallion, learnedly. They were passing their hands over his limbs, wonderfully slender, but strong as iron. They were telling what great deeds would be done by Little Beaver, now that he had in his possession a horse so marvelous.

And that turned the talk upon Thunder Moon, and upon his shame, and upon the dreadful sacrifice which Big Hard Face had made in giving away all of his horses, saving his own war horse, which he had slain with his own hands and left lying before his tepee as a sacrifice to the gods to avert their anger.

Would that sacrifice of all the horses suffice to win back to Thunder Moon the manhood which he had lost?

There were shaken heads. Thunder Moon was a born coward and a disgrace to the Cheyenne name and race. Nothing could be done for him. He would never catch the eye of Tarawa, though Big Hard Face had done a thing which would be famous forever!

Thunder Moon listened, and his heart shrank within him. Then he dragged himself on, and set his teeth to stifle his sobbing.

He had come down to the village with no plan in mind, but now he had a definite goal before him. He would steal, if he could, the fine rifle which was his, from the lodge of his foster father. He would steal, also, one of his foster father's horses, which had been given away on this day on account of shame. Thus equipped he would ride forth. He would find the Pawnees. He would die doing some splendid thing.

He trembled with enthusiasm and went forward with a clearer mind and a more earnest purpose until he came to the tepee of his foster father.

It was dark and silent. He raised the flap with the greatest caution, and peering within, he saw a single dark-red eye watching him. It was the last coal in the dying fire, and by it, at last, he saw the bowed form of White Crow, hooded in a robe.

He was startled at the sight. How could he have guessed that that withered and malicious hag cared for him enough to mourn in this manner for his shame?

He saw, furthermore, Big Hard Face sitting by the fire, bare to the waist, covered with war paint, his arms folded, waiting.

Thunder Moon well knew that, after a time, the great warrior would rise and go forth; and on the warpath he would attempt to show that all honor was not lost to the tepee of Big Hard Face.

And here by the entrance to the tent lay the body of the strong chestnut stallion which was said to be the father of all the chestnut race with which Big Hard Face had blessed the Cheyennes. Here was that very stallion which, with incredible daring, the warrior had stolen from that far land. He was old, now, this doughty stallion, but almost as swift and as strong as ever, and he would follow his master like a dog. Now he lay dead before the lodge.

And Thunder Moon knew that the heart of his father was utterly broken.

Chapter Ten

The greatness of such a grief was overwhelming to young Thunder Moon. He had always known that his father loved him; now he saw that it was a love that counted all the joys in the world as nothing, compared with his joy in his son.

He took a bold step.

He felt that the fixed stare of the warrior was lost in infinite distance, and he, entering softly, would surely be unnoticed. So he glided inside the tepee, and like a shadow he reached the familiar place where his ammunition pouches and his rifle lay. The touch of them sent a thrill through him, in memory of that glad day when for the first time, he had brought back honor to the house of his father.

He raised the rifle. Strength as of steel entered his heart, and he stepped softly back to the entrance. Then he turned and glanced at Big Hard Face, and he found that the burning eyes of the Cheyenne were following him steadily. But not a word passed the lips of the veteran; not by a gesture, did he bid the boy to stay.

Outside, Thunder Moon paused and, with his eyes closed, drew down a few great breaths. Then he stepped across the fallen body of the horse and went back by the very way in which he had come. He felt that he had equipped himself with some manhood, but to make him man, complete, he needed to have that same glorious animal which was now in the possession of Little Beaver.

"Sunset," they had called the horse when it was still a little colt, because in it the chestnut coat had turned to a deeper and a richer red. And he, Thunder Moon, had loved the colt from the beginning. It was a fiery young creature; but while it was still a yearling he had gentled it.

That was four years before. And ever since, Thunder Moon had worked and labored over the magnificent horse until the sight of its starred forehead meant more to him than the sight of a blazing diamond to a miser.

So he crept back to the lodge of Little Beaver and lay down to wait. Hours and hours, with a truly Indian patience he waited, until the excited family group retired to the lodge, having admired their new treasure sufficiently.

Another hour or more he delayed; then he stepped to the stallion and touched it. Sunset turned his magnificent head and sniffed joyously at his young master, but never a sound did he make. For hours and hours, and for months and months, Thunder Moon had labored to teach the great stallion the value of silence. Never had there been a lesson more richly repaid in the learning than this one.

He untied the lead rope. He strapped a saddle on the sleek back. Then he glided on in the lead, and the great horse followed him, stepping panther-soft through the night.

On the outer edge of the village, he paused with a shudder of dread, for an outcry had burst forth in the town. No, it was only a clamor of dogs which presently scattered and then died out.

Then he leaped up into the saddle. He settled the rifle and the ammunition pouches. Yonder passed the slowly drifting shadow of the outer patrol. He waited until the rider had gone well by and over the next dip of ground; then he jogged Sunset forth into the night and beneath the bright faces of the stars.

An owl hooted almost at his shoulder. He turned and regarded, silently and calmly, the dim shadow which sped on, close to the ground. He had no doubt that this was a message from the Sky People; and furthermore, he had no doubt as to what it meant. They had sent the dismal owl forth to tell him that their eyes were upon him, and that in this journey he would surely die.

He could have smiled. He was certain that death was before him; he only wondered that he could be so calm, and that there was no tremor of his nerves as he faced the world of darkness.

Always, before, he had dreaded to venture out beyond the limits of the village; but now it seemed to him that the darkness was a kindly thing because it would cover him from the prying eyes of men. The stars burned wonderfully close, so that he could look up to them and imagine the lighted tepees of the streets of heaven where the warriors feasted and boasted all night long, and prepared, unwearied, to ride forth the next day to the fields of the chase and to the battle.

In some manner, he had been brought close to those people who dwelt in the regions above him. Perhaps it was the greatness of his weakness which had made them pity him and take an interest in his welfare; and the passage of the owl, a little before, assured him that even now they had been speaking of him, and had sent down their mournful messenger to bid him prepare for death.

But he was prepared already; and as he looked up to the shining of those stars, he told himself that surely the bright ones in their happy city above had granted to him a brave man's death to redeem his shame.

He looked back, in his mind, to the silent, darkened tepee of Big Hard Face. He saw that lodge thrown open. He saw Big Hard Face striding joyously down the village street, and greeting his friends, and receiving their congratulations, because the news had just come that Thunder Moon had died gloriously in battle, as a good Cheyenne should do!

There were no tears of self-pity in the eyes of Thunder Moon as he thought these thoughts and brightened the blank field of the night with these paintings of his imagination. Rather, the calmness and the sense of strength increased in him, momentarily.

Then he was aware of a greater blackness on the earth, and a dimness in the heavens. Dawn was commencing.

He found a water hole, unsaddled the horse, and turned it out to graze, while he, himself, stretched out on the earth with one ear pressed against it, sure that if horses galloped that way, his senses would give him warning, and waken him in time to saddle Sunset and then be off. And, once started, let even the swiftest follow him! He would show them how Sunset could run, with a boy's weight in the saddle! He laughed a little, and fell asleep.

When he wakened, the sun was barely up. He was wonderfully rested, and he looked about him on the prairie with a perfect content. It was no strange place to him. It was to be his deathbed, in a day or two, he felt, and therefore no sense of loneliness oppressed him.

"I shall kill one man, at least, before I die," said Thunder Moon to himself. "Surely, the Sky People will grant me that much glory!"

The thought consoled him. Afterward, his scalp would dry in the lodge of some Pawnee, perhaps; but let that be. Tomorrow would take care of itself.

In the meantime, that he should be strong for his first and last battle, he must have food.

He walked out from the place where he had slept, rifle in hand, mind at peace, nerves quiet.

What would the Sky People give to their condemned warrior? They would not forget him, surely!

He had barely topped the next swell of land when something flashed in the hollow beside him—the tail-disk of an antelope. The next instant, there was nothing but a dun-colored streak, as the little speedster darted away to safety.

Thunder Moon jumped the rifle to his shoulder, swung the muzzle with deadly bead on the fugitive for an instant, and fired.

He lowered the rifle. The antelope was still running with gigantic bounds, but he had no doubt of the result. That bullet had cleft the heart. He knew it with a perfect surety. And at once, in answer to his expectations, the little animal bounded into the air, and fell back dead upon the ground.

He spent two hours in preparing the body, taking the best portions of the meat, and placing them over a slow fire to dry. Then the sun burned brighter and hotter and helped the fire.

By noon, he was equipped with dry meat for his journey. His horse was thoroughly fed and rested. He, himself, was at ease in body and soul and he felt a curious lifting of the heart as he faced forward, in the afternoon, to the completion of his adventure. It was almost as though his soul were detached from his body; and from a distance he looked down as a spectator and wondered what the death scene of this young Cheyenne should be.

But nothing happened that day, or the next, or the next; and traveling in a straight line all the while, even though he kept consistently within the strength of the stallion, he was putting many miles behind him. He was voyaging far off into unknown regions. And yet, his nerve did not fail him; for when a man has resigned himself perfectly to death, what else is there to frighten him?

On the fourth day, he looked down upon, what he felt certain, was his death scene. He had guessed it, indeed, the instant that he saw the dust cloud in the distant sky, traveling with a greater speed than even stampeding buffalo can attain. He knew it more certainly, when his straining eye dissolved the cloud and saw the two bands of riders. The smaller band raced in the lead. The larger followed close behind. They came still closer, and he knew the little knot in front to be Cheyennes; and those behind, Pawnees.

Yes, this was the day and the place where he was appointed to die!

He had dismounted from the stallion at the first sign of the dust cloud, and made the big horse lie down like a dog. Now, he prepared to mount and enter the battle.

Chapter Eleven

Battle, perhaps, was a misnomer. Battle there might have been, but it could not have lasted long; for in the group of the flying Cheyennes there were only five braves, and behind them rushed at least a full score of the Pawnees. Their wild whooping echoed across the prairies and came to the ears of the boy.

He marked them calmly. Yonder man with the many feathers in his headdress—he should be the victim to fall by the rifle of Thunder Moon, if the Sky People were willing that so great a glory should fall to the hand of a maiden warrior!

And after that—what mattered?

He looked to the loading of his rifle. He found it prepared; and now, at a word from the boy in the saddle the great horse rose to its feet.

There had been a low growth of brush screening them.

Now, as they rose above it, he saw that the plight of the Cheyennes was not as bad as he might have feared. They were holding back their horses, close to the Pawnees, and yet their mounts seemed fresher and fuller of running. Only, the rearmost member of the party rode upon a staggering pony. Its flank was crimsoned, and the boy knew that an arrow or bullet must have struck it.

To save that member from death, the other four in the band repeatedly reined back and presented their bows and sometimes even launched a few arrows; but in spite of this, the Pawnees were pressing closer and closer, and in a few hundred yards, at the most, they would be on the unlucky warrior.

He was no unworthy brave. Thunder Moon recognized him at once as Running Wolf, a hero who had counted *coup* upon his enemies no less than four times, and who had taken three scalps for the glory of his tepee and the Cheyenne nation. Such a hero was not to be abandoned lightly. Now, from time to time, he was seen to turn slowly in the saddle and look back, as though calculating the moment when he should swerve his failing horse around and charge back to a fighting death among his pursuers.

Both the fugitives and the pursuers were so intent upon their game that they were blind to the new horseman who had appeared upon the scene. The rifle of Thunder Moon was presently at his shoulder, and his bead followed that befeathered chief who seemed the principal figure among the Pawnees. He drew the trigger; the explosion kicked the gun butt back into the hollow of his muscular shoulder; and he of the feathers, without so much as a death cry, pitched from the saddle and rolled headlong on the ground.

At the same instant, Thunder Moon shrilled forth his war cry and sent Sunset forward with a bounding stride, loading his rifle with lightning rapidity as he went.

Where was fear now? He did not even think of it. To stand like a brute and receive the knife was one thing; but to rush down to battle, venturing death, was only a consummate joy to Thunder Moon. Or was it a new and heaven-given self which the Sky People had placed in his body for this great day? He only knew that he was winged with fierce strength and with happiness. He knew how the eagle feels as it stoops on its prey; and straight at the little horde of Pawnees he drove his course to strike one more blow among them and die.

Behold, they scattered like a dust cloud when a changing wind strikes it. Each man sought only to save himself. For the Indian loves to surprise, but he hates to be taken unawares; it destroys his morale at a blow.

Moreover, did it not seem utterly impossible that a single brave would dare to charge them? They heard the explosion of a rifle. They saw their leader in the dust, a dead man. They saw his galloping horse rush far ahead with lightened saddle. And then they saw a Cheyenne yelling the war cry of that nation, rushing down upon them with triumphant speed!

They did not stop to look again. Right and left they veered, preparing to escape the shock of a great war party led by this single bold chief; and Thunder Moon found that he was let straight through the center of the band.

Just before him, a huge man, last of the band to move to escape, was turning his little pony with frantic haste; but as he did so, he grasped what had happened, and his shout boomed heavily against the ears of Thunder Moon.

"Pawnees, are you fools? This is only one child who attacks us! He shall die. His scalp shall dry in my tepee."

And swinging his pony straight around, he drove at Thunder Moon, drawing his war bow as he went.

A rifle exploded on either side of Thunder Moon, and then a second gun spoke on his right.

Well, let death come if it would; in the meantime, this was an easy shot before him. In his practice days, he would have scorned to select, as a target, a man-sized object not ten yards away.

He did not even raise his rifle to his shoulder, but fired it point-blank, at the Pawnee, from the hip.

The latter dropped his bow and clutched the mane of his horse; and Thunder Moon, passing, struck the naked shoulder of the brave with the barrel of his rifle.

He had counted *coup!* Most glorious of all, he had

counted *coup* while charging single-handed through a solid body of the enemy!

Now there were no Pawnees before him, and Sunset was bearing him away from them with wonderful speed in the direction of the Cheyennes, to where Running Wolf, having captured the passing horse of the Pawnee leader, was swinging into the saddle.

What necessity was there of death, now?

Thunder Moon looked back in amazement. It could not be that this glory was to be given to him, unpaid for. Yes, for there were the Pawnees barely recovering now from their alarm and gathering again to make head in the pursuit, while Sunset bore swiftly and safely away from them; and the Cheyennes before him, their throats strained with yells of joy, set their horses at a gallop again.

Another moment, and Sunset was striding amid the fugitives, and the whole party was making excellent headway over the plains. The superior quality of their horses told in the race at once. In vain, the Pawnees screeched behind them. The following voices began to die away; then suddenly they stopped. Thunder Moon, looking back, saw that they had veered away and were trotting their beaten ponies back toward the distant spot where their two dead men lay.

At the same moment, following time-honored Indian tactics upon the plains, the pursued checked their mounts, jumped to the ground, and loosening the girths, led the ponies slowly along, to cool them off and allow them to recover their wind in preparation for any new emergency which might arise.

Running Wolf hastened to the side of the boy.

He caught the hand of his savior and cried, his ugly face contorted with joy and wonder:

"Look on me, Thunder Moon! Tarawa sent you to help me. And the tepee of Running Wolf is your tepee. His guns are your guns. His horses he keeps only because he hopes Thunder Moon may ask for them. His squaws are your servants and his children are taught only one thing from dawn to dark—the name of Thunder Moon!"

The boy raised his free hand to the blue of the heavens, and to a crystal-white cloud which was blowing across its face. With what wonder, and gratitude, and joy, he followed the passage of that cloud!

"The Sky People told me what to do. They raised the rifle and fired it. They replaced the load and fired it again. Give your thanks to them, Running Wolf. But I—I am only a woman among the Cheyennes!"

They had been long on the warpath, these braves; and therefore they could know nothing of his shame, and he said bitterly:

"I stood on the eastern hill facing the sun and Big Hard Face gripped my flesh and raised his knife; but at the first touch of the blade I screamed like a girl and fell down. I am only a woman in the tribe all the days of my life."

His head fell on his chest which was heaving hard. And Running Wolf walked on beside Sunset with his hand still holding that of the boy, and his face averted, lest he should look upon the shame in the eyes of his rescuer.

There was such tact among these heroes of the plains as many a drawing-room could not boast. Not one of the other four needed to be told his duty; but each dropped his head and studied the ground upon which he walked rather than embarrass the boy with the weight of his glance.

Then Running Wolf began to talk from the fullness of his wisdom and from the stores of his knowledge; for wise he was, though he was young. North, and south, and east, and west, he had ranged on horse-stealing raids, and on the warpath. His herd of horses was among the largest that any single Cheyenne owned. In his tepee four squaws worked busily to bead his deerskin suits and to prepare his buffalo robes. All that the heart of an Indian could desire was possessed by the young brave, and in his excursions he had picked up enough information to fill the brain of any one man with Indian lore.

And now he said:

"In the lodges of the Pawnees there was a strong brave. The war ponies bent at the loins under his weight. When he stood on the ground, he pitched a stone five strides beyond the strongest of the other Pawnees. Now this man is dead. Thunder Moon was stronger than he. Is Thunder Moon a woman?"

He made a little pause, and his hand tightened a bit on the slender hand of the boy.

Then he continued:

"In the lodges of the Pawnees where there are many clever horse thieves and a few brave men, the bravest and the wisest was Three Feathers. When he rode out on the warpath, he was followed by the strongest warriors of his nation.

"His horses he numbered by twenties. He had five squaws in two lodges, and many children.

"He was so wise that when he stood up in council, the medicine men bowed their heads and listened.

"He was so strong that seven scalps hung in his tepee. His clothes were bordered with scalp locks.

"Three Feathers is dead!"

There was a sudden and fierce shout of exultation from the other four Cheyennes. Thunder Moon saw the glint of the battle fire in their eyes.

"Three Feathers is dead. He was strong and wise, but he was not so strong and wise as Thunder Moon. Tell me, then, is Thunder Moon a woman?"

There was another brief pause; and then in a stronger, wilder voice the brave chanted:

"There is a man among the Cheyennes. He is not the poorest in the nation; neither is he the greatest fool. He has counted a *coup*. He has stood up in the council and told of the scalps he has taken, and no man has called him a liar.

"He has led parties on the warpath. He has taken many hundred horses from the Pawnees and from others. The Crows and the Blackfeet know his name!

"But this man's life was thrown away. It lay like a pebble on the ground.

"Thunder Moon picked up his life and gave it back to him.

"Tell me, then, if Running Wolf is a woman? And yet Thunder Moon is stronger than he!"

Chapter Twelve

There were what might be called extra reasons for the extreme joy of Running Wolf over the events of this day. He had been off on a long voyage across the plains, into the regions of the distant Blackfeet; and there he had hunted well for horses, plunder, or scalps; and yet, despite all of his skill, he had been forced to come back, at the last, without any token of the time and labor which he and his companions had invested. Altogether, it had been a very bad business, and it would ruin, at a stroke, his fame as a leader and as a dashing warrior.

They would, even, have been run down by the hardy Pawnees, when a bolt from the blue had appeared in the form of a thirteen-year-old boy from the tribe who had been shamed among the Cheyennes as a woman. This boy had scattered the Pawnees, killed the famous Pawnee war chief, and one of the leading warriors, and had placed in the hands of Running Wolf a fine horse which carried at the saddlebow a good rifle, the five scalps of which Three Feathers had boasted, and above all, the medicine bag of that great fighter!

This, at a single stroke, was enough fame and plunder for any expedition to win. From the dark of disgrace, from the depths of the most imminent danger, the band had been rescued and lifted to an eminence. Now, no matter how long the history of the tribe might endure, they would never forget how Running Wolf came into camp upon this day, riding the horse of Three Feathers, with the captured scalps and the medicine bag as a trophy. All of these things, by right, belonged to the boy, and he should have them. But the glory of taking them would rest with Running Wolf's war party.

When he thought of these things, was it any wonder, then, that his heart swelled with the most profound gratitude, and that he looked upon the advent of the youngster as a gift from Heaven?

He and his followers would have gibed at the weakness of this child under torture as much as any of the braves among the Cheyennes. But now, they were willing to sing words of a different tune.

He called one of his followers to him.

"When we come into the city of our fathers," said he, "and when the children and the young men see this boy with us, and honored by us, they are apt to laugh at us and at him before they hear what he has done. And the first man who laughs at him must become my enemy and yours. Therefore, you must ride on ahead. Do not spare the whip. Do not rest till you come to our city. Tell them what has happened. And when we arrive, they will know that Thunder Moon is a man indeed, though he may have failed like a woman when he saw the knife in the hand of his father."

"And what if they ask me to explain?" said the warrior.

"Tell them how he scattered twenty Pawnees like twenty sick dogs," said the other. "That is enough explaining. Only go, quickly."

So, with that word, the messenger took his horse and disappeared across the plains, while the rest of the party voyaged more slowly after him.

But when they came in sight of the city, the heart of Thunder Moon failed him, and he stopped Sunset.

"I cannot face them, Running Wolf," he said. "They have heard me scream like a child when I saw the knife. They saw me fall to the ground. How shall I be able to look into their eyes?"

"Do you not understand?" said Running Wolf with some fervor. "The Great Spirit knew that at this time I should be traveling across the land. He saw in the future how the Pawnees would hunt me, and how the arrow would wound my horse. He knew that there was only one

Cheyenne who could save me. And if you, Thunder
Moon, had been in your father's tepee, caring for your
wounded breast, I should have been lost! So he devised it
all. He shamed you before the people, so that he could
make you glorious, afterward. Tell me, Thunder Moon, is
there any other way of explaining these things? Tell me,
when you stood on the hill and faced the sun, did you not
feel the hand of Tarawa making you weak as a woman?"

Weak, indeed, Thunder Moon had felt, but he could
not attribute it to Tarawa and the rest of the Sky People.
He knew that if he faced the knife again the same weakness would come upon him, and that there was something
lacking in him which all the rest of the tribe possessed.
He could not despise pain as they did.

He had no chance to turn the matter over in his mind,
however. For here was Running Wolf riding beside him,
his hand on the shoulder of Thunder Moon, when a rout
of men and boys and girls, riding their fastest ponies,
swept out from the village and tore across the plains toward them.

Thunder Moon would gladly have turned rein and fled
at full speed, but he could not leave that kindly hand of
the warrior. And before he could think again, a screaming
horde of excited people had broken around the war party
like rapid waves rushing around a rock. The noise deaf-
ened and almost blinded Thunder Moon. He saw Running Wolf hold up the captured scalps and the medicine
bag, and he heard a scream of joy from the multitude.

For in the medicine bag was something even more important than the scalp of the great Pawnee. There was literally his soul, which could never depart in happiness to
the far Hunting Grounds, to ride across the pleasant blue
fields and course after the phantoms of the buffalo which
had died on earth. And if that medicine bag were destroyed, the soul of Three Feathers would be destroyed
also, and wander, forever, without rest.

No wonder that the Cheyennes yelled with joy; for too
many of their families had lost members when Three
Feathers took the warpath.

The pandemonium grew. The whole rout pressed slow-

ly on toward the town, and then the whirling mob divided
a little, and before the eyes of Thunder Moon appeared
the most dignified figure of the tribe—Lame Eagle in person, riding upon a magnificent black stallion, and dressed
in his full regalia as a chief.

"He has come to forbid me to enter the city except on
foot, like the dog that I proved myself to be on the hill
when I faced the sun!" thought Thunder Moon.

He would have checked his horse, but he was suddenly
too numb of brain and body to make a movement. And
now Lame Eagle was just before him. He raised his hand.
Silence swept over the multitude, except for the snorting
and the trampling of the horses.

"Running Wolf," cried the chief, "you are welcome to
me because you have come back with glory, after making
fools of the Pawnees; but better than that, you have found
us a new warrior. He shall be the greatest among his people. The Blackfeet and the Crows, the Comanches and
the Pawnees, shall sleep lighter than wolves because they
know, now, that we have with us Thunder Moon."

He said more than this, but a delicious mist of happiness pervaded the soul of Thunder Moon, and he could
not hear the rest.

He hardly knew what was happening; but presently
they all moved slowly forward toward the village, and the
noise recommenced and reached a vast crescendo as they
reached the outskirts of the village, where the dogs joined
in with their barking and howling.

"Let us go first to the lodge of Little Beaver," said
Thunder Moon to Running Wolf.

"Go wherever you will. Every lodge in the nation is
open to a great warrior," said Running Wolf, who had
been worked up into a frenzy of joy by this huge recep-
tion.

So they turned aside and reached the tall lodge of Little
Beaver.

That chief, barely returned from the hunt, was in the
act of springing into his saddle again, when he saw the
procession come toward him.

Thunder Moon jumped hastily down, and taking Sunset by the bridle, he led the stallion hastily forward. It was impossible for his anxious eyes to read the face of Little Beaver. Time and ferocity had so marred the features of that warrior that no human expression could possibly work its way to the surface. But before him Thunder Moon stopped and extended the lead rope.

"Tarawa told me to borrow this horse from you, Little Beaver," he said, to cover up his theft in the best possible manner. "He needed to send me far away on a fast horse, and so he told me to borrow this one. Now I have brought him back to you. Look at him and make sure that he is not lame and his wind is still good. And there is your saddle, also, on his back!"

Little Beaver jumped in turn to the ground. He seized the lead rope, and glanced hastily over the big horse.

"It is true," said he, "that the Sky People have given you this horse; and therefore what am I, to take him from you? Take him again, and the saddle on him, and only remember to pray that Tarawa may look on my son with favor and make him as brave and as successful as Thunder Moon!"

He replaced the lead rope in the hand of Thunder Moon, and the latter climbed back into the saddle in a daze of joy. He had not dreamed that the thing could turn out in this manner. But here he was, restored to more than good standing in the tribe, and the stolen horse given to him freely!

He looked anxiously at Lame Eagle.

"Is it right?" he asked.

Lame Eagle smiled.

"It is right, friend," said the war leader. "The gods have given you that horse. You will have more and more glory riding him. And if Little Beaver tried to take him back, he would stumble and throw Little Beaver over his head. I have seen such things happen! Be sure that Little Beaver would rather point a gun at his own head than to ride that horse after you have made it yours!"

And they turned, with the whole procession, into the heart of the village.

Chapter Thirteen

They went first of all, as though by mutual consent, straight toward the tepee of Big Hard Face; and that famous fighter they found standing in front of his lodge. It was no longer the lodge which Thunder Moon knew. That tepee had been a huge and handsome one, covered with fine paintings of buffalo, and hunting and battle scenes; but this new tepee was a ruinous old affair. At the very first glance at it, Thunder Moon knew what had happened. At the same time that Big Hard Face had given away all his splendid horses, which were the apple of his eye, he had also given away all of his other possessions. Even the lodge which sheltered him had been made a present to some friend; and now the house of Big Hard Face was simply a battered and patched and staggering old wreck of a leather tent, hardly large enough to shelter two dogs, let alone two people.

The buffalo robe in which the celebrated warrior was wrapped, was a mere flea-bitten rag of leather of which even a boy might have been ashamed. There was no rifle in his hand, but only an old war bow, greased up, and put into service.

At the very first glance, Thunder Moon understood that Big Hard Face felt that the disgrace of his son had been the result of the judgment of the gods, and that to propitiate those mighty powers he had straightway given away all that he possessed and reduced his wigwam to an empty shell. He had undone all of his lifework, and the lifework of White Crow, also. Such a vast sacrifice choked the throat of Thunder Moon, you may be sure.

All of the possessions of that warrior of the terrible

face, were not worth the price of the rifle which Thunder Moon carried in his hand! For all of that, it seemed to him that Big Hard Face, in the midst of wealth and envied by all the other Cheyennes, had never been half so noble as he was now, in the midst of his poverty.

There was no need for Lame Eagle to say:

"Behold your father, Thunder Moon! See what he has done! Out of the greatness of his grief for you, he has given away everything. He has given away such a wealth in horses as no Cheyenne ever possessed before. He has made himself poorer than the poorest Cheyenne, to see if such a sacrifice would change the minds of the Sky People and make them good to you. Tarawa did change his mind. He sent you glory and courage and strength such as no Cheyenne boy ever before showed in battle!"

Lame Eagle went a little before. He led the great charger, Sunset, with one hand; with the other, he led Thunder Moon. Behind him came Running Wolf, leading the Pawnee horse; and the other warriors of the party followed, and all the other inhabitants of the village pressed up behind them.

Lame Eagle knew exactly what gracious words to say at a time like this, to make happiness more perfect. He said in his strong, and deep, and gentle voice, which penetrated into the soul of Thunder Moon and remained there forever:

"Oh, men of the Cheyennes, look well and remember this! Here is a father who would lay down his life for his son, and who first laid down all his possessions. The Sky People saw, and relented. They saw the good that was in the heart of Big Hard Face, and they saw the sorrow that was in the heart of Thunder Moon. They made that young warrior suddenly great. They made his eye like the eye of an eagle. They made his hand like the hand of two men. He went from us, he took a swift horse, he journeyed all alone across the prairie.

"There was no one to guide him! There was no old friend to advise him. Who was there to say to Thunder Moon: this is the best trail, or this way leads to the water hole? No, there was no one.

"But he was not afraid. He went forth all alone, and he laughed at the prairies and called them his friend, because the prayers of Big Hard Face were working for him.

"Then, because he had the eye of an eagle, he saw a great distance off, that many Pawnees followed five warriors of our people.

"There were many, many Pawnees. They were like a herd of buffalo, thundering across the prairie. Their feathers sang in the wind. Their horses ran like running fire. Nothing could stand up before them.

"But Thunder Moon was not afraid.

"He stood up and made his great horse stand up. He took his rifle. He would not aim at the little men. He aimed at the greatest man in that band of Pawnees. That was a famous warrior. Twenty times we have heard his name, and it has always been at the head of a war party; twenty times Cheyenne women have wailed and children have wept because of Three Feathers; but the bullet of Thunder Moon went through the heart of the chief!"

There was a wild yell of exultation from the tribesmen, and they leaned forward and followed the narrative of their chief as though they were hearing the story for the first time.

"Yet that was not enough!" cried Lame Eagle, losing his calm dignity in the excitement of his speech. "There were many Pawnees like a herd of buffalo. They had lost only one man. They had only to run a little farther and they would trample down one of the greatest of our braves, a famous man, a man who has taken many scalps, a man who is a boast and a pride to the Cheyenne nation —that man was Running Wolf!"

Running Wolf straightened and folded his arms—not in vainglorious pride, though to be so praised by the war chief was a thing to be recounted to generations of descendants—but, rather, to show that he was the man spoken of, to let all see his face and the resolution which was printed upon it.

"The horse of Running Wolf died with every stride it made. And Thunder Moon saw.

"He was a young warrior. Some would have said that he was still a boy.

"He had done enough. He had done more than most of us accomplish in a long life, with that skillful shot. Still he was not satisfied. His heart was great. There was a god in him. He called to his horse, and the horse leaped forward. He yelled his battle cry, and the sound of it drove like a knife through the heart of every Pawnee. They saw him coming. They were filled with terror. They turned to the right hand and to the left—all except one man.

"For there was one man who did not have fear. He was a famous man among his people. Spotted Antelope was his name. Where he rode, many Pawnees would always follow. He was rich with the plunder of his enemies. He did not know what fear was, even when he saw Thunder Moon rushing down upon the battle!"

Thunder Moon had hardly heard the beginning of this narrative, so great had been his grief, and his joy, and his pity, at the sight of his foster father. He had studied the face of Big Hard Face, and he had seen not a trace of emotion upon that battered mask of humanity.

But now the story, which Lame Eagle told, stirred the heart of Big Hard Face and set his eyes to burning, and the heart of Thunder Moon was set on fire, also. Never had there been, since the beginning of the world, words of such sweetness as those which he spoke in praise of Thunder Moon.

The pick of the Cheyennes stood about to listen. The hearts of the young men were filled with wonder and envy, and the little children who had once scorned Thunder Moon, now wished only to be praised like this—and die!

No wonder that the spirit of Thunder Moon took wings and soared in his triumph, as Lame Eagle continued in a ringing voice:

"So Spotted Antelope remembered all his greatness and his strength. And he saw that this Cheyenne who came upon him was young, though he advanced to the battle like flame running on the prairie.

"Spotted Antelope turned his horse. He thought to

gain for himself great glory, and to be remembered for avenging the death of his chief, Three Feathers; and he hoped that he would hear all the Pawnees praising him for this deed.

"He rushed to meet Thunder Moon. He raised his rifle. But Thunder Moon shouted, and the noise of his voice smote the ears and the heart of Spotted Antelope. He sat like a dead man in the saddle. He could not move. Then the bullet tore through his heart and he fell down to the earth; and darkness closed over all his war trails, and his battles, and his fame, and his strength. At that moment, the grief of the Pawnees began to rise from the earth like a cloud of dust, blackening the face of the sun.

"But Thunder Moon swept on. He took the finest horse among the Pawnees. He gave it to Running Wolf. Thus he saved the great chief from death, and brought him safely back from the battle, and gave him again to us—together with the soul of Three Feathers!"

He pointed. Running Wolf raised the medicine bag. The screech of the Cheyennes smote the heart of the hollow sky.

"Be glad, Big Hard Face!" cried Lame Eagle. "You gave away much; but now it is all sent back to you!"

He pushed Thunder Moon forward, and the boy rushed into the arms of his father.

He could not help it. His heart was breaking with joy. He trembled. His face was convulsed and the tears would come.

Suddenly the ample folds of the old cloak were cast around him, and he was gathered against the breast of Big Hard Face, and he heard his foster father saying:

"Peace, dear son. Do not let them hear. Let only your father hear. Because he understands. You are not as others. But you were made by Tarawa to gladden the heart of Tarawa."

Chapter Fourteen

Lame Eagle, the instant he saw the buffalo robe folded about both of those figures, turned about to face the tribesmen and lifted both hands. He did not need to give an order. All understood, and like shadows they melted silently away.

There was something worth marking in the bearing of all of these people. The old men walked with smiles, nodding as though this scene had freshened in their minds memories of the glories of their youth and of their race. The strong warriors in the prime of life went off with eyes on fire, because they had never before heard such words from the lips of Lame Eagle. The young men were so many impatient tigers; some day they, too, would be praised like this. Was not such praise worth death, itself?

But the women wept, and embraced one another; and, as they went slowly away, they whispered:

"Have there not been fools among the Cheyenne women, that none of us would marry Big Hard Face and be the mother of such a son as that?"

The medicine man heard, and said:

"No woman was the mother of that boy. Tarawa set him upon the earth. Go ask of Big Hard Face how he found him in the first place, lying naked on the ground!"

So another link was forged in the chain of the legend of Thunder Moon.

In the meantime, Thunder Moon was led slowly into the tepee of his foster father. They walked like two blind men, until White Crow ran out, with tears flowing fast down her face, and seized upon them, and brought them into the lodge.

There she seated them, and they looked on each other with smiles of love and sympathy, each understanding, in this moment, things of which he had never dreamed before. In the meantime, White Crow, with trembling hands, served them with food from the pot of buffalo meat which simmered over the fire.

After a time, as the untasted food lay before them in horn bowls, a voice spoke before the tepee, and White Crow drew back the flap.

"The men of the Cheyennes have gathered around the fire," said the deep-throated voice of a warrior. "There are Running Wolf and all his followers. They wait to have the dance begin. The drum is already sounding. You may hear it!"

In fact, the rapid, throbbing beat of the drum came like a hurrying pulse across the air, bearing with it vague excitement.

"Tell Lame Eagle," said Big Hard Face, "that we stay in our lodge and open our hearts to Tarawa. My son will not dance. He is tired with glory. He will rest, and give thanks to the Sky People!"

"This is well," said the voice of the warrior, but there was disappointment in it.

His step withdrew, and Big Hard Face said:

"There will be many other days when the warriors will draw for sides and sit in the council tent, and the stick will be passed for deeds to be told and *coups* to be counted. Then, you may tell again what you have done! But let this day be mine. I have been a poor man; now I am counting my riches."

And he looked upward, where the thin smoke from the fire crept up through the hole in the top of the lodge, but could not obscure, in passing, the rich blue of the heavens beyond.

"I have not spoken," said Thunder Moon softly, "and I shall not speak of it. It does not please the Sky People for me to tell of what they have done for me. But now, father, open your mind and tell me the things which I do not know."

"Ask me, my son, and I shall answer if I may."

"In the battle, father, when I saw the Pawnees riding, I was not afraid. I saw them come, with their guns and with their bows, but I was not afraid; I was happy when I rode down on them. But when I stood up on the hill, and faced the sun, and saw the knife in your hand, I was afraid of the pain. I was not afraid to die. But I was afraid of pain. How could that be? How could it be that, though I wanted to be brave, I was a coward? How could it be that I loved you, and yet I disgraced you?"

Big Hard Face lowered his glance and stared straight before him, thinking of the misery of the days which had been.

"We are made, my son," said he, "by a more skillful hand than the hands of women. He knows how to fashion us so that each of us has a strength. Some of us are brave by night and weak by day, and some are weak by night and brave by day. Some are fortunate in battle, but their lodges hold no peace for them. Some are rich and fortunate in their villages, but never count a *coup* in war. All our blessings come from the Sky People, and if they give them all to one man, will he not be like the Sky People, themselves? There will be nothing for him to envy in the sky. Therefore they are afraid to let any man be too happy!"

"That, father, seems very wise and true. But when I think of Lame Eagle, I wonder what sorrow could ever come to him. Surely, he has always been perfect, and wise, and great, and good!"

The warrior smiled.

"Do you think so? Lame Eagle is a great chief," said he. "But he has had his sorrows. When he was a younger brave, and his fame was only beginning, he married a beautiful girl; and she died giving birth to a son. That son lived to be a handsome little boy, then he died also in a summer heat. Those are sorrows, are they not?"

"Ah, yes," said young Thunder Moon, "and that tells me why it is that Lame Eagle is so often grave."

"Yes," said Big Hard Face, "and who can tell how often the heart of Lame Eagle turns after those whom he loved, and who slipped out of his hands, like water or sand."

"Ah," said Thunder Moon, "but what a pity that so great and good a man should have to suffer so!"

"Perhaps his suffering helps to make him great and good," said Big Hard Face. "The things we know, we feel for. If you have never been frostbitten, you smile at the man with a swollen foot; but if you have once been pinched by the frost, you offer him remedies. Perhaps Lame Eagle is so popular because he has suffered even more than most men, and that has made him kinder to them."

"There is old Two Bull Elk, though," said the boy. "He has lost nearly all his brothers and sons in battle; but that sorrow has only made him cruel. He kicks every boy that comes near him, and he snarls at the men."

"Men are like plants, child," said Big Hard Face. "Some have roots that lie only on the surface of the ground, to drink the rain quickly; if you dig around them, you break the roots, and the plant will die. And some have roots that sink deeply down into the earth. Those plants can be cultivated, and it makes the root stronger and the plant richer and greater. So there are men whom troubles disturb and destroy; and there are men whom troubles waken and make stronger and better. Such shallow-rooted men are like Two Bull Elk; and such great and noble men are like Lame Eagle. He would rather see a friend win a victory than win one himself; and I have never heard him speak of his own deeds as he spoke of yours, today. But I have seen him break the battle line of the Blackfeet, like a wind breaking a scattered line of straws, or like you, my son, breaking the line of the Pawnees!"

"Ah," said Thunder Moon, "That was only because I came on the Pawnees by surprise, and they were frightened. They must have thought that there were other men coming behind me, and that they had been trapped. Three Feathers, who might have told them what to do, was down."

But Big Hard Face lifted his head and smiled, and

worshiped this handsome son of his with a long and joyous glance.

"You know already," said he, "that the hero has no wits when the leader is killed. Ho, Thunder Moon, if I were a young man again, would we not ride on the warpath together? Perhaps I still am not too old!"

So they talked together in the tepee, until they began to hear the noise of the drum muffled by many chanting voices, and now and again a long-drawn war whoop thrilling through the air.

White Crow set open the flap of the lodge entrance, and they sat and listened.

It was the dusk of the day. Now, looking to the west, they could see the flames of the fire straining the air with crimson; and now and then, when fresh brush was thrown on the blaze, a great yellow head of flame leaped up and sailed, like a phantom of brightness, toward the sky, only to be snuffed out instantly.

Sometimes the chanting ceased, and there was only the light throbbing of the drum; and out of the distance they could catch the murmur of a single man's voice, shouting a chant. They could easily picture to themselves the eager faces in the massed circle and around the light of the fire, one half-naked brave dancing, with the firelight glittering on his copper body, while he chanted of his deeds, and the great things that had happened on the warpath.

White Crow had taken up a pair of moccasins. She did not need light to guide her skillful fingers; and as she beaded the moccasins, she began to sing. It was merely a murmur which passed like an undertone through the distant noise of the war dance around the fire. The man and boy listened. They were content. They raised their faces, now and then, to the brightness of the stars, and smiled.

Chapter Fifteen

Not much sleep came to Thunder Moon that night; for now and then, when his eyes grew heavy, a fresh wave of joy would rush over him and leave him trembling, breathing short, and wide awake with happiness. Twice he got up, and went to Sunset, and talked to the great horse; and the stallion lowered his head and listened with shining eyes that reflected the starlight; and he seemed to understand.

But at last the gray dawn came. A chill settled in the air. Dogs began to bark here and there, in distant quarters of the camp. A child cried near by. The sharp scent of wood smoke drifted through the air as the noises of day commenced.

Big Hard Face and his son stood up from their beds and went down to the river. They plunged in and swam across to the far bank and back again; then they whipped the water from their hard bodies, with the edges of their palms, dressed, and went toward the village.

On the way, others met them with cheerful, respectful greetings. But one thing impressed young Thunder Moon more than all else.

He passed a youth of fourteen, going with his father and uncle toward the river. The boy pressed close to the older men, and stared at Thunder Moon, and pointed; in fact, he seemed half afraid, as though he were close to some terrible and wonderful phenomenon. Yet that same boy had often cuffed the ears of Thunder Moon, and downed him in wrestling bouts, and beaten him in swimming and foot racing, and mocked at his futile efforts with the war bow!

How their relationship was changed, now!

They reached their tepee. To their astonishment, White Crow was not there. Neither was the pot of buffalo meat steaming above the fire for their breakfast, but the place was empty and deserted, and even the few robes and the war bow, and the other possessions which had remained to Big Hard Face, and the rifle, and Sunset, which belonged to Thunder Moon, had vanished.

"This is very strange," said Big Hard Face. "Hush! Say nothing. We shall soon learn. That grinning woman knows something!"

The squaw at the open flap of the next tepee watched them with a smile which stretched from ear to ear.

"Where has White Crow gone?" asked Big Hard Face.

The squaw laughed heartily, and shook with her mirth.

"Perhaps she has run away with some handsome young Cheyenne. She did not wait to tell you about the marriage. She has eloped, perhaps."

Even the anxious Thunder Moon could not help smiling in turn at this idea as he thought of the ugly, time-withered face of White Crow. However, the loss was very serious, if loss it were. The rifle and Sunset at one blow— it almost offset all the glories which he had won on the trail the day before!

"There is a joke. Act as if nothing were wrong," said Big Hard Face. "All the Cheyennes want to laugh at us. When men praise you today they wish to laugh at you tomorrow!"

That bit of wisdom entered the heart of Thunder Moon, and never left it, thereafter.

They passed a boy, playing with his dog, hitching a little travois on its impatient shoulders.

"Have you seen White Crow?"

The imp looked up with a broad grin.

"She has gone home," said he.

He would say no more, but burst into peals of merriment as they watched and stared at him.

"Tush!" said Big Hard Face, gritting his teeth. "They are making fools of us. If I had so much as a pony, I would ride out and hunt buffalo and forget about them until night. But I have not even a bow, not even a play bow!"

They walked on, in search of their vanished possessions.

Presently, they came upon a greater stir and commotion. The sun was brightening the heavens to rose and pink, now, and all the life in the city was on foot and busy.

A familiar tepee rose before them, its top decorated with the image of a great crimson bear. Well did they know it, for it was the handsome home in which Big Hard Face had lived, up to the time of his disgrace.

Now, both he and the boy paused to look at it.

Thunder Moon sighed and looked quickly up into the face of his foster father.

"Ah," said he, "what a price I have cost you!"

"Do you think so?" asked the Indian. "I tell you, my son, there is no counted price for glory. You cannot buy it with ten horses or with ten thousand. The gods have taken what they wished from me, but it was my sorrow and my prayers that they wanted more than my goods. Do not think of that lodge, for I have already forgotten it!"

But Thunder Moon knew that this was merely a kind lie; for that lodge had been a sort of tribal pride, and if a party of Sioux came to visit their allies, they were sure to be led slowly past the tepee of Big Hard Face, that they might be shown in what splendor a Cheyenne could reside.

They drew a little nearer to the old home, and as they did so, a cry burst involuntarily from the lips of young Thunder Moon; for he saw assembled around the tepee the whole herd of chestnuts, all of those glorious horses which had been the delight of Big Hard Face.

In a dozen years, the descendants of the original four horses, which Big Hard Face had brought from the far lands, had increased to a score and four. The least of them could make a mock of the swiftest and most enduring pony that any other tribe of the plain could boast. The breeding of that herd had been the joy of Big Hard Face—that, and the growth of his son. The growth of Thunder Moon had carried with it as many heartbreaks as joys; but the growth of the herd had been one ceaseless triumph.

He had parted with all of those beauties, and now, as he looked upon them again, a strange sound rose to his lips, and he trembled violently. Thunder Moon regarded him with terror. He had never seen Big Hard Face so nearly unmanned before.

"If they had wings, they would all be eagles, and they would chase all the other eagles out of the round arch of the sky," said Big Hard Face in a broken voice. "Yes, Tarawa would receive them with joy! But they have no wings, so they are only the lords of the earth! They are the chiefs. Other horses are not worthy to follow them!"

As a matter of fact, he was about right. He had received a peerless strain of English thoroughbreds, and he had selected the finest of the stock with a sure instinct; and under his care, on the broad plains, they had grown not less swift, or beautiful, or docile, but infinitely hardier, more enduring, more courageous, with thews of iron and hearts that dreaded nothing. They would face a charging bull, or a maddened band of wolves. One might hunt ten thousand miles, and never come upon another band such as these.

"Look!" exclaimed Thunder Moon suddenly. "There is Sunset among them! What can have happened? Who can have brought all of your horses together? And how did they dare to take Sunset? What can it all mean?"

"Do not ask," said the warrior. "My heart is too full to make an answer. I already begin to suspect—and yet it would be too wonderful to be true. It cannot be!"

They went on, with feet that stumbled in their haste.

They passed through the herd of horses; and as they did so, the beautiful creatures turned their heads and whinnied recognition of their masters. They had been under the care of strange hands; and many of their backs were marked by the pressure of cruel saddles; and they no longer knew the gentle treatment with which they had been reared.

On through the horses they passed, touching sleek flanks and polished necks, until they stood before the tepee and saw, within the flap, White Crow, who seemed to await their arrival.

"You are very late," said White Crow.

Chapter Sixteen

"Say not a word," Big Hard Face cautioned his foster child.

Then he added in a hoarse whisper: "I suspected when I first saw. But I cannot be right. This is earth and not heaven. It is all a joke or a dream. Do we sleep, Thunder Moon?"

They entered the tepee. There was the meat pot steaming over the fire. Thunder Moon spied a dear possession.

"My rifle!" he cried.

He leaped to it.

"Stop!" called Big Hard Face. "Do not touch it. It is in the lodge of a stranger. It is not yours until he admits that you own it. This is all very strange. White Crow, will you gape and gasp like a starved bird in a nest? Or will you open your foolish throat and tell us what it all means?"

"What should it mean?" asked White Crow with a shrug of her shoulders. "Cannot your eyes tell you that you are at home, and that I have been waiting for you long enough?"

"Home?" echoed Big Hard Face. "Home?"

"Bah!" The squaw was impatient with them. "Will you never eat and have done talking? Are the horses to stand there all day and starve themselves?"

"The horses?" echoed Big Hard Face.

"Aye, the horses. Are they to starve?"

"What have we to do with the horses?" cried the warrior, beginning to shake again like a man with the palsy. "What are they to me?"

"Ho?" grunted White Crow. "Then I am growing blind. And I have let them tie the horses at the wrong tepee."

"Certainly you have."

"Then you are not the old warrior, Big Hard Face?"

Big Hard Face threw up his hands to heaven.

"Tarawa, give me patience. Do not let me strike this foolish woman because she lays on me words worse than whips! Foolish White Crow, tell me what it means!"

All at once, the squaw began to weep. She reached for Thunder Moon; and though he could hardly remember in his entire life a single caress which she had given him, now she bent her head on his shoulder and began to shudder and sob.

"Do you not see?" she stammered. "You paid too great a price. You offered the whole of your horses, and everything you owned. But only the life of the first red stallion was enough, the first horse, your own horse, that you carried back with you from the Far Land! The gods did not want them all. They took only that one dead horse. Now they give back to you all the living ones!"

Not even then, could the warrior understand what had happened; but first he walked aimlessly around the tepee and picked up long-familiar things.

The wealth that he had spent his life collecting, and which he had distributed through the entire tribe to his friends, had now been collected again, and replaced in his tepee. There was not so much as a single knife missing— not so much as a single pipe, or horn spoon, or painted buffalo robe, or back rest.

Then, gradually, Big Hard Face knew. He rushed to the door of the tepee, to fling himself out among his horses, to embrace them, to pass his hands over their beautiful limbs and sleek bodies, to call them by their names, to pet them, and love them like a madman.

When he returned to the big lodge, he saw that there were other Cheyennes slyly watching from the entrance of other lodges. He controlled himself and turned back into the lodge.

"Do you see, White Crow?" said he. "It is as I always said that it would be. You told me that the boy had ruined me. I told you that there was more richness in a son than in a herd of such horses. Look! On account of him, I lost them; on account of him, I gain them back again."

White Crow was drying her eyes.

"They are all angels," said she. "All the Cheyennes are angels!"

In fact, it was an occurrence unprecedented in Cheyenne tribal history; for, of the rich gifts of the unhappy warrior, not one had been retained, but all had been returned to this man whose foster son had helped to make the tribe famous and dreaded on the plains. The deeds that men do, said Lame Eagle, have a great value; but the deeds that children do are far greater. Whereas a man may have only the strength of his muscle, a child has the help of Tarawa; and muscle is nothing, compared with the strength of the Sky People.

"Go out and run to your friends. Tell them to give you plenty of buffalo meat," commanded Big Hard Face. "Today we are going to make a feast. It will not be a feast to the whole tribe. They shall all come to our lodge, and sit there, and eat, and smoke, in honor of my son, to show that my son and I honor them. We are one people; we are one blood; we are one kin; you and I and all of the Cheyennes! Do you doubt it, Thunder Moon?"

"I, father?" asked the boy. "Are you not my father? Therefore, of course, I am one of your people!"

Big Hard Face started.

Now and again, a pang of doubt seized him, and he felt that perhaps it would have been better to raise this child with the knowledge that he was of a different blood, lest when the knowledge came to him it be too violent a shock and estrange the boy from him.

But now the thing was done and he felt that it could not be undone.

So it was all done, on that famous day, to the great expense of Big Hard Face, but to his lasting honor, and to that of his foster child.

As the feast drew to an end, Big Hard Face said to Lame Eagle:

"Is there any man who would dare to say that Thunder Moon is not a true Cheyenne and worthy of his blood?"

The great chief inhaled a breath of smoke from his pipe and then puffed it toward the sky.

"Perhaps he is even more worthy!" said he.

Chapter Seventeen

White Crow, the old aunt of Big Hard Face, pointed to spots and streaks of white on the quilled robe which was gathered about the shoulders of Thunder Moon.

"White is for life," she said. "That is why I am glad of my name. White is for life; you see that I do not die. White is for life, not for a sleepy and dull life, but for a quick, busy, happy, active life.

"And," she continued, "do you see this light blue, bordered all around with many-pointed stars? That, my child, is the blue of the heavens, and these stars are so many suns. It is a wish that your life may be that many times brighter than the lives of other people. And that blueness means that they pray your life will be serene and peaceful as the heavens are, when the Sky People have brushed all the clouds out of it. Here is green, too, to show that they hope you will always grow stronger, and bigger, and taller, and greater, and never begin to stoop and to bend—like me!

"There is much red, too. One can hardly tell what red means, until one has studied the whole robe. But usually it is a wish for warmth and a good home, with plenty of food, and rich blood always flowing richer in your body. These streaks of amber yellow hope that you may always grow more beautiful and perfect; and the black, of course, which you see here, shows that all the fighting will end, some day, and you will be at perfect peace!"

Thunder Moon, nineteen years old now, was proud of his robe, and he spread out another fold that more of it might be admired; and, in fact, it was a thing of beauty. All its surface was painted and quilled, the designs worked in closely and yet harmoniously; and it represented more hundreds of hours of work, when one considered the numbers of little porcupine quills which had to be sewed on and flattened in place, than one could imagine.

"I have worked on this robe myself," said White Crow. "I have often sat with the women in the lodge of Little Beaver and whitened my hands to keep them from soiling the robe, and I have sewed with them. I am not the slowest woman among the Cheyennes in sewing quills, and neither am I the slowest in beading a moccasin. I do not need much light to work by, either. It is not for nothing that I have decorated thirty-seven robes!"

There was a rumbling voice from across the lodge, and Big Hard Face turned on his heap of buffalo robes, where he had been resting, and said: "Are you going to begin to tell about them all, like a warrior counting his *coups?*"

"Do not listen to him, if you wish to hear about this robe which you have," said the squaw to the boy. "You see that there has been a great deal of work spent on it, and Little Beaver must have had some great idea in mind or he would not have made it a gift to you. I know that he wanted it for himself."

"It was because no other young man among the Cheyennes has counted five *coups,* and killed eight men!" said Big Hard Face, rearing himself to a sitting posture and looking with eyes that blazed with pride upon his foster son. He added with a melancholy afterthought: "There are no scalps; but perhaps there will be a time for them!"

"No scalps," repeated Thunder Moon with equal gloom. "I think that I shall never be able to take one."

"My son," said Big Hard Face, growing excited, for the subject never failed to make him furious, "do you not know that all the enemies who are not scalped may fight with you again in the Happy Hunting Grounds? And then you will have to kill them all again—if you can! But those who are scalped cannot go up among the Sky People. They would be laughed at, having no hair on their heads.

After a while, their spirits rot away like their bodies. They are no more. The wolves pull their bones to pieces, and the spirits of those men fall apart and can never be put together again!"

"You have told me all that before," sighed Thunder Moon.

He leaned his chin upon one fist. With the other hand he drew out a hunting knife, long and brilliant of blade, and heavy of shaft. He began to toss it with a flick, so that the point stuck into the post that held his saddle, war accouterments, medicine bag, and headdress. It was only a short distance; he could reach out his hand again and pluck the knife forth. But the trick consisted in driving the knife every time into one thin seam in the bark of the post. And the steady hand never failed.

"I have told you all of this before," said Big Hard Face, "but a young man must listen fifty times to his father; and then, more. He must listen a hundred times, until he has learned the truth of the lesson. And you, Thunder Moon, have never learned!" He grew more and more excited. "Why should you kill them, then? It is only fighting with shadows, unless you take their scalps also."

"Or their medicine bags," put in White Crow defensively. "For he has taken three of those!"

Thunder Moon looked up a little hopefully, but the face of his foster father was darker than ever. He said: "What scalps hang in our tepee except those which I have taken? And when the stories and the stick pass around the circle, if it is asked what scalps have been taken, my son sits silent. He has never taken one. He has nothing to say, and no glory is brought to our home."

"But when they count *coups!*" exclaimed the squaw. "Ah, that is a different matter, is it not?"

"Five *coups* are much, and eight dead men are much, also. But where are the scalps? Where are they?"

"I cannot tell why it is," said Thunder Moon, deeper in gloom than ever. "But I have taken a dead man by the hair and caught my knife in my hand. But always my hand grows weak. I cannot use the knife. Suppose that there were life in him! Suppose that he were to groan under the cutting edge of the knife!" He dropped his head, suddenly, and raised a mighty hand before his face to shut out the vision. Big Hard Face glowered at his ancient aunt, and White Crow bit her lip and turned her head away, so that she might not view this sign of womanish weakness in her nephew.

"Listen to me!" cried Thunder Moon.

He leaped to his feet. The robe fell from him and revealed six feet of such masculine beauty and might as could not be equalled in all the heroic race of the Cheyennes. The eye of Big Hard Face glittered with satisfaction as he noted the rippling of those muscles.

In only one fashion could the marvelous beauty and strength of this figure be improved, and that would be by changing the sun-browned darkness of the skin to a still darker hue, tinted with a red copper color. However, nothing can be perfect. We must take what goods the Sky People send to us and not grumble too much for what they have forgotten to give.

"Listen to me, my father," cried Thunder Moon. "I have sat in the circle and seen other men join in the scalp dance, while I was forced to be quiet, like a woman. This shall not be any longer. I am going to take out a band of young men. I am going to lead them on the warpath. I know what ones will follow me. I am not considered a woman among the young men of the tribe. They will follow me. I shall not take too many, so that there may be more prizes for the ones who ride with me. And when we come back, we shall all have scalps. We shall not return without them!"

White Crow threw up both her hands.

"See, Big Hard Face! You drive him out to be murdered by the horse-stealing Pawnees, or by the wild Comanches!"

A single glance from the older warrior silenced her. He stood up in turn. There was nothing but the utmost satisfaction in his face.

"What is the age of Thunder Moon?" he asked.

"He has been nineteen summers with us," said White

Crow, eyeing the heroic form of the youngster with wonder and love.

"I have not heard before," said Big Hard Face, "of a brave taking the warpath as a leader at that age. Are you sure that men will follow you, Thunder Moon?"

The young man smiled a little, not boastfully, but because his satisfaction could not be entirely concealed from the others.

He said: "Yes, there are some who will follow me. Many of them, I shall not take. I shall not pass the pipe in a crowd, and accept whoever would ride with me to pick up glory as a dog picks up scraps of food which others have left. But there are a few men that I have marked down, and them I shall permit to ride with me."

Big Hard Face smiled in turn, with infinite content.

"My son," said he gently, "is it truly your purpose to find scalps, and to take them, and bring them back, that the souls of our enemies may dissolve like dust?"

"It is," said the boy.

"And do you know how to begin?"

"I know, but I should like to be told again, so that everything may be done right."

"Then go to some wise man. I could tell you. I have told other men how to lead a party. But you, go to some friend and ask him."

"To what friend shall I go, father?"

"To the wisest and the best man that you know."

Thunder Moon picked up his robe and threw it carelessly over his shoulders. He drew upon his feet a pair of finely beaded moccasins. He took up his hunting knife, dropped it into the sheath, and with his long staff in his hand he stepped forth from the tepee.

He paused and looked about him; and from the lodges near by, since it was the evening of the day and most of the warriors had returned to their tepees, many a head was turned toward him.

Above all, half a dozen boys, who were wrestling and laughing near by, stopped their games, and turned to gape at the tall figure of the youthful warrior.

He made a sign. The whole group of youngsters sprang instantly to meet him.

"Which of you will carry a message to a friend for me?"

"I!" cried every pair of boyish lips.

He smiled down on them. Of all the stern young braves of the Cheyenne tribe, he was the only one who could spare time from the pursuit of honor, to romp and play with the children. He loved them, and they regarded him with a mixture of affection and awe such as men and children usually reserve for familiar gods.

"There is something for each of you to do," said he. "You go to Yellow Wolf, and you to Snake-that-talks, and you to Young Hawk, and you to Big River, and you to Standing Bear. Tell each of them the same message. I wish to see them all at moonrise, at the edge of the river. Tell each of them not to fail. It is very important. Now, which one of you will deliver a wrong message?"

"If I make a mistake," cried one of the youngsters, trembling with eagerness to serve this god, "I shall tear off a strip of skin from my shoulder to my wrist, in honor of Tarawa."

"That is enough," smiled Thunder Moon.

He waved to them, and they were away like so many dogs, each flying along a different course, each furious with zeal to please his patron. Thunder Moon watched them out of sight and laughed pleasantly to himself. Then he went on through the village.

He paused to admire the tepee of High Hawk. It was fast nearing completion now, and the bands of decoration had been brought almost to the edge of the ground. A whole group of men and women were gathered here, to wonder at the beautiful quillwork of stars and concentric circles, and all the fine colors with which it was furnished, and all the paintings, enough to make a legendary history of the family which was to occupy the lodge.

And as he went off, he heard the shrill voice of an old woman saying: "When Thunder Moon takes a squaw, what manner of lodge he will build! That will be a thing to travel ten days to see!"

Yes, plainly the tribe was well pleased with him, in spite of this matter of the absence of scalps, which irritated his father so bitterly. So he went on, more content, until he reached the lodge of Lame Eagle.

Chapter Eighteen

The tepee of the war chief stood toward the center of the village, and Lame Eagle himself was at the entrance to his spacious lodge, examining, in detail, a horse which had been presented to him that same day. It was a beautiful, cream-colored mustang, perfect in every part. Thunder Moon stood by and admired it in his turn.

"You have come to tell me if this is a good horse, Thunder Moon," said the chief, "because you know all about horses."

"My father knows," said the young man modestly. "I only remember what I have heard him say. But if you wish me to speak of this horse, I should say that he would be good for hunting buffalo. But I would not ride him to battle where the race might be a long one and where there are not apt to be many other horses to change to."

Lame Eagle frowned a little at this unpleasant news.

"Why do you tell me that? I was given fifty horses to choose among, and I chose this cream-colored horse."

"He has a good color, and he will not sweat soon," said the boy, "but his shoulders are not good. They should be more sloping. Do you see how upright they are? Note also, that he is too rangy, too long of back, too light in the loin to pack much weight. He would carry a boy or a small man very well. But he will be ruined if he runs very far under your weight."

The war chief turned, and the feathers in his headdress nodded at the youth. The frown presently vanished from his face.

"You are a truth teller, Thunder Moon," said he. "And

some day you will grow so wise that you will know only old men. No others are able to put truth in the stomach and grow fat on it!"

"I don't understand what you mean by that," protested Thunder Moon.

"You will remember it some other day, however," said the chief. "There is White Rain. He looks sad today, does he not?"

The medicine man went by with a long stride, muffled high about the face in his robe, so that only his hooked nose and his burning eyes showed above it.

To the war chief he raised a hand in salutation, and then he passed on.

"He did not see me," said Thunder Moon grimly. "I have brought him more presents than any ten of the other young men of the nation, and yet he does not see me, Lame Eagle. Can you tell me why?"

"He grows old," said the chief, "and old men sometimes see only their own thoughts."

The young brave smiled, as grimly as before. "That answer," said he, "went around a corner before it came to me."

Lame Eagle shrugged his shoulders, as he saw that he would have to give a clearer explanation.

Then he said: "Where shall we talk?"

"It is serious talk," remarked Thunder Moon.

"Then come with me into the tepee."

They went in together. The chief sat opposite the entrance, his guns beside him, enjoying the comfort of the back rest, and let his eyes wander over the splendor of the furnishings, until his eyes raised to the exposed trophies —the scalps which had been taken by this Achilles of the plains.

They were fifteen in number, and the *coups* which the hero had counted had been over twenty. As for the dead men who had fallen before him, their number could only be guessed at. Then the glance of the youth reverted to the sinewy hands of Lame Eagle, and his heart swelled suddenly and sternly in his breast. For if it came to a matter of single combat, then he told himself that he would not fear Lame Eagle. No, he would not fear him by day or night, on foot or mounted, with knife, club, bare hands, or rifle; besides, what man in the nation would dare to confront Thunder Moon with the war bow, which he had been so long in mastering, but which at last he had made such a perfect servant? He squinted his eyes a little and thought of it in his father's lodge, made of toughest horn, and half an arm's stretch longer, and much thicker and stronger than this bow in the tent of the war leader.

Yes, when it came to battle, he would stride as far in the face of danger as this man, and he told his heart of hearts that long before he reached the age of Lame Eagle, he should have far passed the mark in trophies which that fighter had established. Not that Thunder Moon was entirely vainglorious. For he knew that sheer might and cunning of hand did not make a great chief.

"Will you take the pipe?" asked the chief, reaching for that instrument of solemnity.

"Let it be as if we had smoked," said the boy. "I do not wish for the pipe. Tell me first, Lame Eagle, why White Rain hates me so much?"

"You have not been able to guess that?" smiled the leader.

"No."

"We shall eat, and then we shall talk."

Thunder Moon hastily swallowed a morsel of the food which was offered to him by a diligent and attentive squaw.

"I am filled with my own thoughts," said he. "Let us have talk. And tell me first about White Rain."

The chief first took the pipe; and having filled and lighted it, he blew a little puff of smoke to the ground, in manner of libation to the earth spirits, and another into the air above his head, in honor of the Sky People. After that, he began to smoke quietly, half closing his eyes in enjoyment.

But he was even more thoughtful than contented, and from time to time, as he talked, his glance flashed keenly to the side and studied the expression of his young guest.

"Of all the young men of the Cheyennes," said the

chief, "there is one who is far the wisest, and who can think long thoughts beyond even the grip of the oldest men, and who can pass many bright pictures before the eyes with his words, and who always has an answer. But among the Cheyennes there is one who is also as blind as a newborn child. Some things he does not see at all, and what lies just before him is less known to him than what is over the hill!"

"And who are these two men?" asked Thunder Moon, bright with curiosity.

"They are both one man," said the chief. "They are you, Thunder Moon!"

The latter winced under the double thrust and caress of this speech. He was surely unlike the rest of the young men and the old ones of the tribe, in that he could only partially mask his emotions. They were usually written clearly enough—too dimly for a white man to have followed them, no doubt, but plainly enough for the keen glance of an Indian to see through at once, from a distance.

"I am that man, then," said Thunder Moon. "And White Rain hates me because I am blind? Is that, then, the reason?"

"Do you not fear that White Rain may have blinded you, my friend, being unfriendly to you?"

Thunder Moon laughed shortly in contempt.

"I think that White Rain may do very great things," said he. "He may bring down the rain, of course, as we have all seen so many times. And sometimes he does other tricks which are curious to watch. But as for blinding me, or changing me in any way, he has not the strength, Lame Eagle. He simply has not the strength. Each man's mind is its own place, and is surrounded with a wall higher than the blue sky, and no other man may climb over that wall."

"Now, then," said the chief, "you have explained the matter for yourself."

"I don't understand how."

"But you know that all the other young men in the

tribe dread White Rain worse than the guns and the arrows of the Pawnees or the Comanches."

"Yes, that is true. I have laughed at the way they cringe before him, like beaten dogs."

"And consider, Thunder Moon, that the medicine man has seen your laughter! Is not that enough to make him hate you?"

"But," exclaimed Thunder Moon, "if he has such a power, he should prove it to me. He should convince me. I am ready to follow him and to think him a great man; but surely first I have a right to make him prove what he can do. I pick up this knife. I say: 'White Rain, I dare you to keep me from throwing this knife into that post!' "

"Hush!" exclaimed the chief. "He will hear!"

"Bah!" sneered the boy. "He will not hear. He cannot hear farther than you, or than I! White Rain, work magic and big medicine and make this knife miss the mark, if you can. Make it turn in the air and fly back at my own breast!"

"Do not throw!" cried Lame Eagle, tense with excitement, the sweat standing out on his forehead. "These are dangerous words, my friend!"

"Look!" laughed the youthful brave.

His sinewy arm went back and flashed forward with incomparable grace and speed. The knife shot in a twinkle of light across the lodge and was buried inches deep in the stout tent post.

"Look!" laughed Thunder Moon, while the knife hummed like a savage snarl across the lodge. "Look! Did he stop me, my friend?"

Lame Eagle started up and crossed the lodge. He leaned and examined the knife.

"Draw it forth, Lame Eagle!"

"No, no!" said the war leader. "I would not touch it for the price of ten horses. Who can tell if White Rain has not already worked a spell that will wither the next arm that touches this handle?"

"Let him work his spells to make rain—and wind," scoffed the boy. "But he must learn a new sort of medicine before he can touch my weapons!"

He crossed the lodge, drew out the great knife with a single wrench, and examined the blade. So truly had it been hurled that it had flown in a perfectly straight line, and the cutting edge had not been turned in the slightest degree.

He thrust the knife back into its scabbard, made of brilliant lizard's skin, a trophy taken from a Comanche warrior the year before, when Thunder Moon rode south.

Then he saw Lame Eagle wiping the perspiration from his forehead and shaking his head back and forth in dismay.

"Ah, my son," said he, "you are placing yourself needlessly in danger!"

"It will not shorten my life a day!" exclaimed Thunder Moon.

"And yet you ask me why White Rain hates you, my friend? For this very reason! He knows that you despise his medicine. Is not that enough?"

Chapter Nineteen

Thunder Moon stood, amazed.

"I had not thought of that!"

"No, my son, for you are the blind man of our nation! Besides, did you not quarrel with White Rain once, very bitterly?"

"No, I think not. I am sure not."

"Think again. You forget. There was some trouble between White Crow and White Rain."

"Ah, I had almost forgotten. That was three years ago. He had threatened to put a spell on White Crow for some little thing she had done that displeased him. I only went to him and told him that men should not fight with women, and that if he worried White Crow with his foolishness, I would have him out of the lodge before the whole nation, and show them that his bag of tricks was not worth one dog whip, and a strong hand ready to use it.

That may have angered him, but the next day he met White Crow and told her that there would be no spell."

The chief stared with bulging eyes.

"Yet you wonder why he hates you, Thunder Moon?"

"Why," said the boy, "I have given him three whole buffalo, since then, and a painted robe—because it pleased my father. And as for the other, I had forgotten that. I don't wish to keep my mind filled up with little things!"

"Ah," murmured the chief, behind a dim cloud of smoke. "You do not know, my son, that the Cheyennes never forget! You have not remembered, but be sure that he has, and will, till the day of his death."

"Well, that is explained," said Thunder Moon, "and now I shall pay no more attention to him. I was only puzzled. But now I see that you are right, and that he will always hate me. It will not keep me awake at night, I promise you! But one thing you say sticks in my mind. You say all the other Cheyennes remember—but I forget. And then my skin is brown, and your skin and the skins of the others are darker and redder. Does it mean that I am different, really, from all my brothers?"

The chief frowned and hastened to turn the subject.

"What are differences of skin, when the heart is the same?" said he. "Do not think of that. But who has been putting such ideas in your mind?"

"Nothing. Nothing that I can remember. Except that there are many things from which I am shut out. No soldier societies, for instance, have asked me to join with them, though they are glad enough to have me ride with any of them on the warpath!"

The chief answered diplomatically: "You have honors enough, Thunder Moon. And all men respect you. But in the soldier societies men make sacrifices of themselves. They strip skin from their bodies in honor of the Sky People. They pierce and torture themselves to bring good luck on the warpath. And they know that you would never do that to yourself!"

"Why should I give myself pain?" asked the young

man. "Let my enemies do that! Let them do that, if they can!"

"There is a certain amount of suffering allotted to each of us by Tarawa," said the chief. "And if we give ourselves that pain, we escape taking it from the hands of others. Further, we please Tarawa and the others, because they see that we submit ourselves to their judgment and admit that they are greater than we."

Thunder Moon frowned dark as night and looked impatiently upward.

"There is something above us," said he. "But why the Sky People should be pleased by pain I cannot tell. They are happy people. They should be pleased only by happiness. Sorrow and agony darken their dwellings in the sky. However," he added with a sigh, "you have told me a great many things that I wished to know. You have explained to me why it is that I live outside the lives of all the Cheyennes. And I am lonely, Lame Eagle. I wish to be one with my people. I wish to join in their dances, and to know all their secrets. And though I cannot see why a dead man is made more dead by losing his scalp, I am going on the warpath, and I am going for scalps, with my chosen friends. I have come to you, tonight, to ask what I must do. I wish to make my father happy. I wish to make all of the Cheyennes happy. I wish to obey all of their laws, this time, and not my own pleasure. So tell me everything, if you will!"

Lame Eagle breathed forth a great cloud of the smoke, and, with a deeper note in his gentle, even voice said:

"If I had ten men like you to follow me, Thunder Moon, I would beat the Comanches across the great southern river. I would drive the Crows and the Blackfeet into the snows of their mountains, and I would take the scalps of all the Pawnees and make their women and children our slaves. There would be no tribe that dared to face us. Therefore, Thunder Moon, I wish to see you greater and greater. You have a hand that strikes and you have a mind that thinks. And as for these little things of flayings and self-torment, we shall forget them. You will make yourself such a great glory that no man can question. I shall tell you what to do. You shall fulfill all of the customs of the people, and even White Rain will see, in time, that you are a good Cheyenne."

And he said after a moment: "Have you selected your soldiers? Have you passed the pipe for men to say whether or not they wish to follow you?"

"I have sent a message to each of the men I wish. They will meet me tonight, at moonrise, on the edge of the river!"

The chief smiled a little at this confidence.

"Are they many?"

"There are enough to win much glory. They are not too many to divide it."

"Twenty young men and a few seasoned warriors, then?"

"There are five young men."

"And you will do some great thing with five young men?"

"You may smile, Lame Eagle, and it does not anger me, because I know that you are my friend. However, you shall see what I bring back!"

"Yes, I shall wait to see. Now, in the meantime, get ready to do these things: Prepare to make an offering to the medicine arrows—tail feathers of eagles are the best. Have you any of those?"

"I took a great quantity of them from the Pawnees last year."

"That is true. Then take the tail feathers of the eagles. Your father will tell you how many make a good gift to the arrows. Put on a robe with the hair side turned out. Fill a pipe and leave your lodge, walking slowly, because a man who goes to face the gods must have time to think as he walks. Then you must begin to mourn in a loud voice—mourn for the troubles in which you stand, and, because you want more glory than you have, mourn so that the Sky People will understand that here is a warrior who wants help."

"I don't like that," sighed Thunder Moon. "However, I shall do everything as you say."

"That is well, my son. When you reach the door of the

arrow lodge stand there and wail. Then the keeper of the arrow lodge will come out and invite you to enter, seeing that you need the help of the medicine arrows. When you go in, place the pipe on the ground in front of the arrow keeper, and then step around to the side of the lodge, taking great care, always, that you never pass between the medicine arrows hanging at the head of the keeper's bed, and the fire. The arrow keeper will then take the offerings in his left hand, put the palm of his right on the ground, and pass the right hand down on the offerings. Then he will change hands and repeat this thing, as the wise men of old days have directed, to call the attention of the medicine arrows.

"After that, he will return the gifts to you, and tell you to tie them to the arrow bundle. While you are tying the thong, do not hurry, because before the knot is tied, you must finish praying aloud and telling the arrows all that you wish—horses, or scalps, or other plunder, for if these things have all been done as I direct, the arrows cannot help hearing every word that you speak while you are tying the knot, and if you have done well, the arrows will grant at least a part of your prayer and let you and your men come back from the warpath happily, with blackened faces. After that, you will smoke a pipe with the lodge keeper, and with any others who may happen to be there. That finishes the ceremony.

"Or if you wish, instead of this, you may go away from the city and spend three or four days without food or water, under the hot sun, lying on a bed of sage and—"

"No, no!" cried Thunder Moon. "The first way is the best. Let the tortures be kept for the war."

"Aye," said Lame Eagle gloomily, "and if you fall into the hands of the Comanches or the Pawnees, you may be sure that the Sky People will not take pity on your pain and give you a quick death!"

Chapter Twenty

Down by the river, the face of the rising moon stretched a long silver image across the pool, and out of the darkness of the banks it lifted the silhouettes of six men. One was Thunder Moon, and the others were the men for whom he had sent; for not one of them had failed to come to him.

They were all much alike, as six tall and strong young saplings in a forest. Yellow Wolf and Snake-that-talks could sit in any assembly of men and talk with pride of the scalps they had taken and of the *coups* which they had counted. But they were furiously eager and zealous for more. As for the other three, each of them was as formidable as the first two, but fortune had not placed them in the path of great enterprises so often. They had shown their mettle, and now they were like dogs straining at the leash, wild to be off in the hunt for glory.

All of them were well known to Thunder Moon, as he was known to them, for his deeds, his *coups,* his wisdom to which even old men would listen, his rash courage which made him like a thunderbolt in time of war, and his wealth in guns and horses.

The five had assembled a little earlier than he who had sent for them; and now as he came down the bank to them across the broad face of the moon, the five shadows arose and gave him greeting.

Said Thunder Moon abruptly and earnestly: "Is there any one of you who has a grudge against me?"

There was no answer.

"Is there any one of you," said Thunder Moon, "who despises me or thinks me foolish?"

There was no answer.

"Is there any of you who is not willing to follow me to war?"

At this there was eager murmur. Certainly all were as ready to ride behind this leader as a wasp is eager to find honey.

"Very well," said Thunder Moon. "There are men in our village who say that Thunder Moon is a fool, or else very young, because he has never taken a scalp. And I have made up my mind that I would go on the warpath, and that I would swear never to come back without a scalp to hang at my belt. Listen, and I shall swear!"

He turned to the silver moon, now hanging close to the black margin of the prairie. To her he lifted his arms.

"Bright moon," he said, "you see all things on the earth by night, as the sun sees them by day. You see the owl sail and you see the nighthawk swoop. You see the grizzly bear stalking and the lion stealing through the forest. You see the Indian braves going to serenade. You see, through the smoke of the lodge fires, the faces even of the crying children. Therefore, be sure to see the face of Thunder Moon, and look on down through the smoke of his words and see his heart, and there you will find the words painted, just as they are spoken.

"I have gathered five friends. There are no young men like them among the Cheyennes. There are no men who ride so well, who shoot so straight, or who fight so bravely. They are going to ride forth with me in the search for honor and for scalps. Let us have good fortune, oh, moon, because I intend to try such things as no Cheyenne ever attempted before. I intend to do a thing which will mark this year and set it apart from all the other years of the Cheyennes. And in token of the honor I have for you, moon, because I was named partly from you, I give you this gift as a sign of the great gifts which I will bring back to you from this war journey!"

And he swung above his head a fine rifle, not two years old, and perfectly sound in all its parts—such a gun as many an Indian would gladly have purchased at the price of half a dozen horses. The weapon left his hand

and flew, wheeling clumsily, with the moon gleaming alternately on the polished sides of the barrel. It fell with a loud splashing into the waters of the river and disappeared.

Not a man among the five young warriors who watched this sacrifice uttered a sound. But there was not a one among them who did not wince, and there was not a one among them upon whose forehead the sweat did not start out. For what one of them possessed such a gun as this which had been idly hurled away? And yet they marveled, rather at the greatness of spirit in the man who made this gift to the gods than they grieved because the rifle was lost to the tribe.

"Look!" cried Big River with a shout of wonder and of triumph. "Look at the answer of the moon to her son!"

All raised their heads, and saw the broad disk of the moon sail into a cloud, not thick enough to dim its light, but rather to catch and magnify it, so that the moon seemed to disappear; and in its place there was a little pyramid of crystal fire in the center of the heavens.

The wind blew the cloud away. Once more the face of the moon looked broad and bright and clear upon the earth.

"I am answered!" said Thunder Moon, in a voice deep with satisfaction. "The rifle has already been carried away by the underwater people and given to the moon! We shall have fortune, my friends. Which of you can doubt that we shall have fortune on this warpath?"

So it seemed to them all, and their eyes glistened with respect and with excitement as they watched their leader.

He continued to them: "Yellow Wolf, of all of us, you have taken the most scalps. You know the ways of our people in war. Then tell me, how do we fight against the Pawnees?"

"By day or night," said the other, "and with little parties or in great armies whose horses shake the prairies. To steal horses or scalps, we ride most often against the horse-stealing Pawnees."

"And the Crows?"

"Against the long-haired Crows and the Blackfeet we make fewer expeditions. They are farther away."

"And the Comanches?"

"Against the Kiowas and the Comanches we ride only in great armies with our best warriors and our best horses."

"Good! And do we never take small parties against them? Do not the young men of the Cheyennes ride out in small numbers to take the warpath against the Comanches?"

"No," said Yellow Wolf, "because the horses of the Comanches are the fastest horses in the world, and they are the best riders. And if a small number of warriors rode far off to the land of the Comanches, might they not quickly be overtaken by the thousands of fast-riding Comanches or the Kiowas, who are their allies? So we ride against the Comanches only in armies. And we would be willing to have those terrible fighters for our friends, if it could be managed."

Thunder Moon said finally: "There would be honor for the young men who rode out against the Comanches— would there not?—rode out in a small number, and journeyed far off into the land of the Comanches, and came back with their scalps?"

"Honor?" said Yellow Wolf, and he shuddered. "Yes, and death also! Because the Comanches have horses which would overtake our best ponies in a day's running."

"Listen to me," said Thunder Moon. "I have chosen the five bravest men among the Cheyennes, and I am going to lead them south and west against the Comanches. Which of you will be afraid to go?"

There was a deathly silence, and each youth looked straight before him.

"Tomorrow," went on Thunder Moon, "I make sacrifice to the medicine arrows; and after that, at the rising of the moon, I shall wait for you here by the river. For each of the five who has a heart for this warpath there will be two fine running horses. Now let us go home and speak to no man. Let us tell no one where we go, except that we are riding south, and hope to find Pawnees first."   •

All of these latter speeches were made to a silent audience; and when the six walked back across the moon-whitened prairie, not a word was spoken, except a murmured adieu when they reached the circle of the outer lodges.

Thunder Moon went on to his own tepee with a cloud over his mind. He had had no doubt of these men, before this time. He had not dreamed that they could possibly fail him. But the reputation of the Comanches stood very, very high, at this time. Small parties of the Cheyennes which had in recent years ventured against the wild riders of the southwestern deserts, had all been wiped out to a man, and only a desert-born rumor had swept back to tell their kinsfolk what had come to them. For that very reason, it had seemed to Thunder Moon that the one great feat which was worth performing would be an expedition against these same famous Comanches, with only a few companions, as he had expressed it, to share the glory.

But the silence in which his final proposal had been received was a severe check to him. He went back toward the lodge feeling that he would have to make the expedition alone. Make it he must, for he had announced his intention of sacrificing to the medicine arrows. But to voyage forth alone on the prairies on a journey of such a length seemed to him madness. For such work he needed the keenest of eyes for the trail, the keenest of wits to read every sign of the changing weather, the keenest of trail sense to know in what direction to ride, and always to keep in mind the clearest picture of the way. Such wits, he knew, were possessed by Yellow Wolf and by Young Hawk, at least, and perhaps by others of these selected men. Them he might trust to bring him into the vicinity of the enemy, and once there, he would be capable of leading them to the attack with credit. Only, for the crossing of the great inland sea, he knew that he was most inefficient. For in that direction his talents did not lie.

So the gloom in which he reached his foster father's tepee was very deep, and it was increased by the scene that met him on his arrival there. For he found Big Hard Face and White Crow waiting for him, with darkened, unhappy faces; and the cause of their gloom stood with folded arms near the fire. It was White Rain, the great medicine man!

Chapter Twenty-one

It was plain that the medicine man had been in the midst of a long harangue. His nostrils still were expanded, and his headdress, which was the mask of a great grinning wolf, quivered with the fury of his last utterances. Yes, it seemed to the youthful warrior whose entrance had stopped the speech, that the very echo of the voice of the man of mystery still hung thick in the air.

White Rain concluded tersely: "Here is the man. Let him know what I have said. For all shall be fulfilled as I have spoken!"

He swept his robe about him and prepared to leave, but as he strode out, Thunder Moon said to his foster father: "I shall accompany White Rain to his lodge and return at once."

"Do so," muttered Big Hard Face, "and with all respect. For he sees that the anger of the Sky People already hangs heavily above you, my son! Speak to him gently. Here—there is our newest rifle—give it to him from your own hand."

But Thunder Moon, as though he had not heard this last speech, turned and hastened from the tepee and his light step instantly carried him to the side of the striding man of mystery. He plucked the robe of White Rain, but the latter continued on his way, unheeding. He plucked again, and White Rain answered in a sepulchral tone: "Let no man speak to me! A vision from the Sky People is even now walking across my eyes!"

They were between two lodges, so that they had entered a deep shadow, and sheltered from observation by that darkness, the iron hand of Thunder Moon gripped the shoulder of the medicine man and whirled him about.

The latter was a man of professional dignity and of professional craft. He ruled by wisdom and trickery rather than outright force, but still he had ridden many a time on the warpath, and his hand on the war bow was as much to be dreaded as any man's. Now, as he was whirled about, he lunged straight at the throat of the younger man with the dull glint of a knife in his hand.

For all the speed of that darting arm, it was seized at the wrist. Fingers with the contracting force of shrinking steel sank into the cords. A twisting pressure ground the flesh of the arm against the bones, and the knife dropped from the nerveless hand of White Rain.

But though disarmed, the medicine man did not wince; for he knew that, except for an offense which the eyes of half the nation had witnessed, no man would dare to strike the official wizard of the tribe with a deadly weapon. And the darkness had covered his thrust at the throat of the sneering youth.

"You have seen a vision from the Sky People, have you not?" said Thunder Moon. "A dark vision, then, my friend!"

And he pointed to the sky, where the dark clouds had suddenly been rolled across the heavens by a changing wind. Behind them, the moon sailed up the long arch of the sky like a ship through a troubled sea.

"Go home, young man," said the wizard. "Go home, and listen to the words which are waiting for you there. As for me, I only know that the gods are waiting in thirst for the blood of Thunder Moon to cover the earth!"

"Liar!" said the youth. "When you speak to me, speak as to your elder, White Rain. For I know the truth of many things which you only pretend to know. This very night I have raised my hands and turned the moon into a white fire. Its roundness was lost, because I spoke to it and it wished to give me a sign. Moreover, the Sky People are my friends. Even now, they have stopped the hand of White Rain on its way to my throat!"

The medicine man, rather unnerved by this speech,

snarled like a baffled dog, but he could not help casting a covert glance over his shoulder at the sailing moon in the sky.

"The Sky People," said White Rain, "keep you for a worse death. In the southland Comanches have sharpened their knives for your scalp. They have asked the Yellow Man to give them your life, and he has promised. This I know. For this reason I have spoken in your father's lodge today. For the Yellow Man is the greatest of all spirits, next to those of the Cheyennes. He has made the Comanches great. Cannot he easily give them your scalp, also?"

"You have crossed me many times," said Thunder Moon. "But I am a tall wolf, and I pay no heed when a sneaking coyote flies across my way. However, my patience is ending. Once before, when you carried your lies to White Crow, I told you what I would do if you bothered me again. As for your magic, it is good to make rain, but for nothing else. It raises a little wind in summer, but never a storm. I despise you, White Rain, because I understand the ways of the Sky People. To me they speak, and to you they never will!" He paused, because at that instant there was a long roll of thunder out of the east. "Listen!" said Thunder Moon, "it is the echo of my voice in the sky!"

White Rain, utterly overwhelmed by this minor miracle, could not help shrinking before the tall form of the young man, and, as he shrank, the other said sternly: "This time again I shall have mercy on you, but see that you go tomorrow and tell them that you have asked the Sky People again, and that they have had only good messages this time. This is to help you to remember!"

And with the full strength of an ample hand, he laid his staff twice and again on the shoulders of the medicine man.

White Rain moaned with rage and with pain, but he fled from the shower without attempting to strike back, while Thunder Moon turned and walked lightly back to the lodge of his father. On the way, the first of a thunder shower began to fall, and before entering the tepee, he stood a moment and raised his face to the sky, and laughed as the little stinging drops hit his face.

"That is the magic of White Rain!" he laughed.

He went into the lodge. He found that the two were waiting there in unabated gloom, and Big Hard Face at once broke into excited speech. It seemed that the medicine man had told them with much emotion that he had news from the Sky People that their son was about to ride away on a distant expedition, and that all would be lost to him, unless he postponed his departure for a fortnight and paid ample sacrifices to the gods.

Thunder Moon listened with a nodding head.

"He knows that I am going on a distant expedition. But does he know against what tribe?"

"That he did not say."

"He has heard only a rumor in the camp, then. This day I went to see Lame Eagle, as you know. However, I walked with White Rain to his tepee. He said that he felt the Sky People were changing their minds, and that their answer would be favorable in the morning when he consulted them again. Have no fear. All is well, and he smiled as I left him!" And Thunder Moon, thinking of the grimace which he had last seen on the face of the wizard, could not help laughing aloud.

And as Big Hard Face studied him, that grim old warrior finally remarked: "The ways of the young are not as the ways of the old. This would have cost any young Cheyenne his scalp in the next battle, when I was first hunting *coups*. But now all is different. Perhaps you are right to laugh at White Rain."

"Ha!" gasped White Crow. "What do you say?"

"Sit with me by the door of the lodge," said Thunder Moon to his father, turning his back upon the squaw. "I wish to have quiet words with you. And silence the woman, and let her sleep while we talk!"

Big Hard Face merely grunted to his ancient aunt: "You have heard a man speak!" And he also turned his back on her.

They sat at the entrance to the lodge, deaf to the mumblings of the old squaw, while Thunder Moon said:

"Father, I am about to ride where war parties of the Cheyennes have never ridden before and returned with scalps and safety! I shall need twelve horses so swift that no other horses on the prairie can compare with them!"

"It is done!" cried the warrior instantly. "They stand waiting for you in my herd with the boy watching them as they graze apart from the short-legged ponies of the tribe. Choose twelve of them."

"Sunset!" said the youngster with satisfaction, "and eleven others. The worst of the herd will be better than the best of the other horses on the plains!"

"Yes," said his foster father with quiet satisfaction. "The worst will be better than the best that the other tribes can find!"

"That is finished, then."

With no words of thanks for the generosity of his father, he hurried on to the next detail:

"How many good rifles have we?"

"Three," said the father.

"I need two for each warrior. I need twelve rifles; for the path is long to the scalps which I intend to take, and the way back is longer still, perhaps. Where shall I find nine new rifles and plenty of ammunition?"

The father pondered. "There are not that many rifles in the tribe—of the kind that you want! Take older guns. I will give you robes to exchange for them!"

"I know! I know!" said Thunder Moon. "I have seen the other guns. The insides of them are red with rust. They kill the man that shoots them more often than the man they are aimed at. The bullets they fire fly wide of the mark. Arrows are quicker and better. No, I shall have to have new guns! New guns! I must have them!"

He struck his hands together and glanced at Big Hard Face in a fury of impatience; but the latter smiled and half closed his eyes.

"Good!" said he. "I have told you my mind. Do now as your wits tell you. I cannot say any more. Besides, I am sleepy!"

And he went back into the lodge to his bed.

But his son remained with his knees hugged in his

mighty arms and his head bent far back, watching the
stars, as they swirled in and out of view through the rifts
in the clouds. Where should he find guns? Where should
he find guns?

Chapter Twenty-two

Yes, as he had said to his father, he did not want the
old guns such as could be found in the village. He and his
father knew that the rifle must be fed oil or grease, as a
horse must be fed grass. But the rest did not seem to understand. They were more apt to worship their firearms
than to take care of them. A rifle was medicine in every
Cheyenne lodge except that of Big Hard Face.

Thunder Moon had thrown away one peerless rifle as a
mighty sacrifice to the moon. On account of that sacrifice,
he was reasonably sure of some success on this expedition, but he believed in helping himself. And good new
rifles he would and must have. Where should he get
them?

If one wanted good furs, one traded with the Blackfeet
from the mountains, and they in turn brought them down
from the distant Ojibways, who lived in the frozen north,
or from the Blood Indians, or the Crees. And if one
wanted colored pottery, or beautiful blankets, one traded
with the Kiowas or Comanches, who had them in turn
from the stately Navajos. So it was with all things. One
went to the source where they were provided, and took
what one wished.

But guns came from the palefaces. And there were no
traders expected for many a moon. Even then, the guns
which they carried were often very poor ones. This year
there had been none which caught the fancy of Big Hard
Face or his discriminating foster son.

However, the traders themselves brought in the guns
from more distant Eastern cities where the white men

lived in numbers which some people said were as great as the herds of buffalo which blackened the prairies for miles at a time. Not that Thunder Moon believed the wild tales he heard about the palefaces. He knew, as any wise Indian knew, that the Cheyennes were the greatest people in the world. However, the palefaces were clever in the production of weapons. They knew how to make heads for arrows, knives, lance points, and above all, guns big and little!

Straightway Thunder Moon determined that he would direct his course eastward, first of all. He and his men would take the rifles that they needed, either by trading in buffalo robes which Thunder Moon would carry with him, or else by theft, or, best of all, by superior force of craft and of hand.

With that determination, which was eventually to have so much influence upon the course of his life, he went to his bed, turned on his side, and was instantly asleep.

The next day he rose, bathed in the river, and straightway started to perform the sacrifice to the medicine arrows which would assure still better fortune to this expedition. As he went slowly to the arrow lodge, he saw the people looking strangely upon him; and he knew that the rumor was abroad that he was about to attempt some great thing. The little boys, particularly, followed at his heels, half delighted, half sorrowful. For they worshiped him with a constant affection.

Thunder Moon, as he tied the gift of eagle's tail feathers to the sacred bundle of arrows, spoke as follows:

"Oh, arrows," he said, "grant me one thing: Let me have good rifles for myself and for my friends. This is the only thing that I ask of you. Consider the eagle feathers. Each of them is stiff and new. They are not frayed, and the edges of the feathers are not turned up, and they would steer you straight through the air even at a distant target, without failing. Therefore, give me the guns which I yearn for—good, straight-shooting guns, with a gleam of oil inside the belly of the rifle, to show that they have been well kept, and that the red devil, rust, has not eaten them!" Such was the prayer of Thunder Moon.

Then he went back to his father's lodge, ate a huge meal, and went to sleep. He slept soundly until the evening of the day, in spite of all of the noises of the camp; and when at last he stood up, he felt that his nerves were calm, and that his heart was eager.

In the dark of the late evening, he bade Big Hard Face and White Crow farewell. He went past the tepee of Lame Eagle, and bade him farewell, also. Then he turned out of the camp and went among the horses.

The boy who served Big Hard Face had already segregated the twelve chosen horses, with Sunset at their head. The saddles were ready for two of them, two more were loaded down with robes, to be used for trade, if necessary, and two more were burdened with dried meat.

It was dark when he reached the appointed spot. For a whole hour he waited and watched the stars printing their images in the uncertain surface of the pool. At length the rim of the moon appeared. But still there were no signs of the five whom he had selected for the expedition.

Half the broad shield of the moon stood above the surface of the earth, and then across it passed a file of five stately forms, walking rapidly. The heart of Thunder Moon leaped in his bosom. Here were his men, true to him in spite of the dangers which he had promised them! Yellow Wolf, Snake-that-talks, Big River, Young Hawk, Standing Bear, clustered silently before him.

Then Yellow Wolf, as the most celebrated figure in war, said quietly:

"We have thought much of your words, Thunder Moon. We fear the long marches across the plains. But we have brought out our war gear. Our war bows, and our arrows, and our robes, and our shields, and spears, and knives are with us. We have trusted to you to find us ponies. But why should we not ride our own horses?"

"Brothers," said Thunder Moon, quivering with emotion, "I do not see you as you stand here. I see you with thinner faces, and with older eyes that have looked on many strange things. I see you with scalps hanging from the points of your spears, and the dust of captured horses rolls back into your nostrils! The Sky People promise us good fortune. Your good luck begins tonight, for these are the horses you are to ride!"

He led them past the next coppice, and there they saw before them the tall forms of the chestnut horses of Big Hard Face. Thunder Moon stood aside and watched their delight. It was well controlled by all saving Big River. He was a poor man. He was known to be strong and to be brave, but his father had not five horses to his name, and Big River had always to ride on pot-bellied, scraggy, worthless beasts. Now he leaped on the back of a mare and went careering with her across the plain, managing her with heel and gripping knee, while he brandished shield and spear and thrust his weapon through imaginary foes.

He came back, with a war whoop shrilling from his lips, and went careering with her across the plain, managing children on the back of such horses, would be heroes and take scalps, and we are not children. Only tell me—how could you persuade Big Hard Face to give up so many to you?"

"The Sky People," said Thunder Moon seriously, "have talked to him for me and opened his heart. I had only to ask, and he gave them to me. Take the horses. Go back to the city. Take your saddles and your bridles. Only mind you in riding these horses that their sides are as tender as the ribs of newborn babies. A touch is enough to make them gallop. A word is enough to make them race. Leave only one thing behind you—your whips, for you will never need them. Treat them as your brothers!"

Five gleaming arrows beneath the moon, they raced across the plain and toward the city, half lost in the dusk; and then five sweeping shadows came back to Thunder Moon. He called them together in brief consultation—a brief one, for they were so wild with joy over the chargers which they were to back on this expedition, that they were incapable of long thought on any subject, even of life and death.

"Snake-that-talks," said he, "you have ridden south, though never so far as the way we must go. But have you talked with the old and wise men of our nation? Is the trail a picture in your mind?"

Snake-that-talks, though young, was already famous for his skill on the trail. There were some Indians who could keep in mind the whole story of a trail, like a memorized book. And each hill, each river, each stretch of sand or loam, each change in vegetation was known to them over vast distances. For that reason they were always at home in the prairies.

Snake-that-talks smiled in satisfaction on Thunder Moon.

"Trust all of this to me," said he. "I shall take you to the great river, if you wish, beyond which the Mexicans live. All the way is known to me and the rivers that we cross and the ways of crossing them! Have no fear!"

"And you, Big River, went east last year with your father to the fort of the palefaces. Can you take us there again?"

"Yes," said Big River. "But do some of us ride south and others east?"

"We ride together to the east, and when we start for the south, each of us will have two new rifles. The medicine arrows have promised them to us."

A yell broke from the lips of the irrepressible Standing Bear.

"Look, brothers!" cried he. "I have six Comanche scalps already at my girdle. Hurry, Big River. Lead us to the east!"

Chapter Twenty-three

When Thunder Moon saw before him the looming outlines of Fort Humphrey Brown, he halted his party and examined the place with care; for, even from this distance, there seemed more solid strength in that place than in all the Indian cities he had ever looked on. And he knew, instinctively, that greater things than White Rain had even dreamed of could be found in that fortress and in the town around it. He prepared to go in alone, because, as he told the others, it takes two men twice as long to accomplish what one man can do with ease.

He would not go in on one of the best horses, because he felt that if curious eyes fell upon one of those splendid creatures, the horse might be taken away from him by the force of numbers. But he had with him, as his own second mount, the worst appearing of all of the chestnuts. It had been born a dwarf, and it had grown to a maturity which was comparatively stunted. Not an inch over fifteen hands, with a belly which was incurably potted, and with a long, scrawny neck and a heavy, ugly head, and with high-standing, bony withers, it looked the very caricature of a horse. And yet it had its fine points. If one could look past the first features and get down to the running mechanism itself, then The Minnow, as she was called, was a truly admirable running machine. Her legs were perfection; and there was much power in her quarters and such beautiful strength in her sloping shoulders, that Thunder Moon had particularly let his choice fall upon her, feeling that she would best be able to support his crushing weight on the long journeys, leaving Sunset free for the brilliant work of battle, flight, or pursuit. She had won her name, in fact, by the fashion in which, as a yearling, she had been able to dart out and away from the rest of the colts, when they raced together across the grazing lands and that ability to dart, as well as to jog quietly over vast distances, she still retained.

But when her master had heaped the buffalo robes for barter over her, and when he got into the saddle himself, with his knees thrust up awkwardly high by the short Indian stirrups, she looked like the very siftings of a very poor herd of ponies.

His shield, his spear, and even his war bow, he left behind him, and he went on into the camp with only one rifle, and his knife. Once or twice, as he drew nearer to the fort, he turned and cast anxious glances behind him, but his party had already vanished on the face of the broad prairie, and he stood alone before the gates of a new civilization.

The nearer he drew, the more massive and wonderful the buildings seemed to be. There was a cluster of wooden structures about the knees of the fortress itself, and above them were reared the heavy walls of Fort Humphrey Brown, with a cannon glistening here and there. He recognized them from afar, by the size and the brightness of the metal, and he knew that these were the thunder voices of which even the most gallant Indian tribes were mortally afraid. Then he came before the gate, and found there a little cluster of men, with rifles in their hands, talking with very loud voices. They called out sharply to him, in the white man's strange tongue, which he could not understand, but presently an Indian appeared. It was a Pawnee; and his very eyes turned fire when he saw a Cheyenne. However, since he was a paid interpreter, he went through the usual formula. He asked what Thunder Moon wished to do in the fort, and when the latter said that he had come to barter buffalo robes for the rifles of the white man, he made him swear that Thunder Moon did not enter the fort with the purpose of seeking out any enemy.

When this colloquy ended, he beckoned to the Cheyenne to advance through the gate; and as he did so, he said: "What is your name, Cheyenne?"

Thunder Moon turned and looked the Pawnee full in the face.

"If you knew it," said he, "you would hide your head in a hole the rest of the day, like a prairie dog when the hawk sails over him."

Well pleased because he had come out best in the encounter of words, he passed on through the gates and found himself in the town itself.

He drew The Minnow to a halt before he had gone a hundred yards; for so many new things were rushing upon his senses that he could not very well grasp them all at once. There was the voice of the place, above all. It was not as noisy as an average Indian village, he thought, and there was a great difference in the quality of the sounds which he heard. In an Indian town, all was helter-skelter, and careless, and pointless. There were the wailing of children, and the howling and barking of dogs, and the ring of laughter, and the snorting and neighing of horses —all in a wild hubbub; but in this place, the noises, on the whole, came not from human throats. There was rather a deep, humming sound, blended with a few shrill notes, though even these were not uttered by lips. He passed a darkened house of which the big doors were opened; and, inside, he saw the fierce light of fire, and a man standing with a piece of white-hot iron on which he beat with a hammer, shaping the metal rapidly to his will. A bellows squeaked and moaned under the hand of a boy who helped the blacksmith.

He passed on to where many smaller hammers were tapping at the sides of a house, fastening on strips of wood and building it a thousand times stronger than any Indian tepee.

Then he passed a sawmill on the edge of the river, and he looked in and beheld the great circular saws sinking through the logs which were fed to them, with deep, nasal whines. But these were only samples; and everywhere such sights and sounds flowed in upon him, that it seemed to Thunder Moon that every person in the town was working.

He had heard that among the palefaces even the chiefs were not ashamed to labor more than women; and he had also heard the Indians despise that custom, and he himself had often curled his lip when he heard of it. But it seemed to Thunder Moon that there were differences between this sort of work and that of a squaw. Here was a labor of swift creation which was thrilling to watch and thrilling to think of. Five years before, Fort Humphrey Brown had not been so much as dreamed of; but now it seemed to be rooted in the soil, so that it was impossible to conceive of time or misfortune destroying it.

A horn sounded just down the street.

He reined The Minnow to one side of the street just in time to avoid a column of riders that swept around the elbow turn.

There were fifty cavalry troopers, with jingling sabers at their sides, and well-kept carbines thrust deep into the leather holsters; and, in addition, each of them carried two of the newly invented revolvers.

Their horses were not like the matchless chestnuts of his father, but, still, they were all big, strong, and well-groomed. The men were all dressed in uniforms and everything about them seemed perfectly kept, and perfectly efficient. At their head rode a splendid figure upon a beautiful horse; and each of the troopers behind him kept his eyes straight forward.

Each was part of a machine, it seemed to Thunder Moon. Each had submitted himself to the loss of his free will, had made himself into a cog or a lever, or a tooth of a great destructive mechanism. Suddenly the boy understood why it was that often a thousand Indian braves, no matter how gallant, were not able to break the ranks of even a small group of fighters such as these.

He watched them out of sight, until the dust cloud which they had raised had melted away and left the air pure once more.

Then he turned around with a sigh, and his eyes met those of a tall man who leaned upon a rifle at the side of the street—a man in deerskin clothes, richly fringed. He was smiling half in amusement and half in contempt at Thunder Moon. But something made the latter draw himself stiffly up in the saddle, and he rode past the white man with his head turned, looking boldly and steadily into the eyes of the latter, and giving him glance for glance.

The smile of the trapper went out. He scowled and gripped the barrel of his rifle with a significant force. Yet it pleased Thunder Moon that he had been able to extinguish that half-contemptuous and half-hostile smile.

He went on down the street until he saw something which made him stop The Minnow with a word which was almost a shout. Then he turned in the saddle, and resting his left hand upon his knee, he stared, with mouth agape, at the greatest treasure that it had ever been his good fortune to see, upon a greater treasure than he had even so much as dreamed about.

There was a long awning before a store, the open interior of which was heaped up with all manner of goods, and from which a strange mingling of smells came forth to the nostrils of the boy. Yonder, he could spy the colors of bright clothes, and the glint of many sorts of metal.

But all of this was as nothing compared with what he saw directly before him in the front of the store; for there were exposed, under the care of a guard who constantly marched up and down with the most vigilant demeanor, all manner of arms from rifles to revolvers, and from axes and hatchets to knives of every conceivable size.

A blur of madness swept across the brain of Thunder Moon. With these things in his possession, he felt that he could master the entire world of the plains. Pawnees, Comanches, all the world of red men would go down before him.

Yet what a prodigious fortune would be required to pay for such weapons! Or, if not fortune, what a tremendous exertion of power, to burst into this fort, and reach this store, and carry away these most desired treasures!

However, this was the place to see whether or not he had with him enough buffalo robes to buy nine rifles and ammunition, and he dismounted to make inquiries.

Chapter Twenty-four

When Thunder Moon went up the steps to the store, The Minnow would have followed him, but he stopped the mare with a word, and went on until he was opposite the racks of rifles.

"What will you have, my friend?" inquired a voice in the tongue of the Sioux.

He looked up sharply, glad to hear one speak in the language of that nation allied to the Cheyennes, and, as he did so, he saw a fat, wide-shouldered man approaching. No, the fellow was not fat; that was all muscle which bulged beneath his coat. His long arms dangled far down, and he walked with a springing step. He had the air, too, and the sharp, steady eyes, of a man who is sure of himself.

"Rifles," said Thunder Moon, and held up his fingers to indicate the number.

The storekeeper looked at the tall youth, and then at the ugly-headed, pot-bellied mare which the latter was riding.

"Here!" said he.

He led the way inside the store, past the racks of shining new weapons, and to a corner where there was a group of perhaps a hundred guns standing against the wall.

"Choose among these!" said he.

Thunder Moon picked up one, glanced down the barrel, and handed it back. He looked at the others.

"These are not the ones," said he.

It seemed to him that the face of the white man fell a little.

"All these guns shoot strongly," said the trader. "All of these guns have already been handled by famous warriors!"

"Yes," said Thunder Moon, "and all of those famous warriors are now dead! And perhaps these guns were buried with their masters for a while?"

The trader stared at him, amazed. Then, with a broad grin, but in silence, he conducted his client to the front of the store, and pointed to the new stock.

"And what about these?" said he.

Thunder Moon picked up one and then another. He could not help a grunt of delight. One by one, he selected nine rifles. When he had laid them aside, he went to the mare and lifted from her back the load of robes under which she was staggering. He spread them out on the floor of the store porch. Every one of them was of the finest manufacture of which the Cheyenne women were capable. And every one of them was a painted robe, which might have served as a museum piece.

The trader, who knew that he could take in a fat sum for each of the pieces from Eastern patrons, ran his eye over the list of them and again glanced at Thunder Moon.

So much wealth had never before been brought to him by such a young man, and yet he could see that this was not a chief, nor even the son of a chief; and certainly this was a man who had never taken a scalp.

As for the rifles, they were good ones; and though they had cost the trader a scant third of their usual wholesale price, owing to certain clandestine relations which he had established with an army commissioner, still he wanted to get something like ten times their actual value.

He pushed to one side four of the rifles.

"The robes will buy these four guns," said he.

"Only four?" said Thunder Moon.

The trader scowled.

"Are not each of these guns big medicine?" he demanded harshly. "Are they not guaranteed to take a life every time they are fired in a battle? Do they not shoot straight and never fail? Yes, they are a gift, for such a price!"

Thunder Moon looked at him; and then returned to the mare and brought in his last articles of trade.

These were two new suits of deerskin. They, also, were of the finest manufacture, and they were covered with beads. How many hundreds of hours had been spent upon the decoration of these garments it would have been hard to guess, but certainly the trader had never seen finer costumes in his life. He laid aside three more rifles.

"Here is the price," said he. "What else have you?"

And he scanned the saddlebags of the mare with a hungry eye.

"Is not this enough?" asked Thunder Moon.

The trader scowled again.

"I have offered to treat you," he said, "as a father would treat his son. Here are seven such rifles as you have never had in your tribe before—all new, all strong, all in good condition, and then you would ask me for more!"

Thunder Moon sighed bitterly. He had ten rifles, now, counting the three he had brought from home; but his heart was set on having, not the rifles only, but also plenty of ammunition, as well. For of what use were the guns, unless he had enough powder and ball for his men to practice with on their long march to the south and the west? He was familiar with such marksmanship as was to be found among the Cheyennes, and he knew that practice is the only thing that makes perfect with firearms.

"I have nothing more," he said.

Once more the trader measured the lines of the mare.

"Is she fast?" he asked.

"Yes," said Thunder Moon, "but she is not to be traded."

Not even his dire need could make him part with any of the priceless chestnut blood.

"Not to be traded," said the keeper of the store. "But would you bet on her speed?"

"Bet on her speed?" smiled Thunder Moon. "Yes, of course!"

For betting was a thing with which he was familiar. He could remember the day when Little Beaver had betted away all of his possessions, even down to his squaws. That day, Little Beaver had gone to sleep, a penniless man. The next morning, he borrowed a horse, and with that for a beginning, he had such fortune, that by the night he had won back all that he had lost and more besides. Any Indian would bet up to his last penny with a cheerful countenance.

"You have now seven rifles," said the trader, hastily gathering in the robes and the beaded suits.

"Yes," sighed Thunder Moon again.

"I will bet you those against seven more rifles, and run a horse against your mare. Will you do that?"

"Gladly," said Thunder Moon. And he would have laughed, except that he remembered that at such times it is best not to appear too sure.

"How long is the race?" he asked.

The trader glanced once more to the mare. He wanted to make assurance doubly sure; and as he noted the high withers, and the scrawny neck, he made sure that though she might possibly possess the endurance of the Indian pony, she could never possess sprinting speed.

"From here," he said, "to the edge of the gates, and back again. Are you contented?"

Thunder Moon measured the distance, likewise. Over a short stretch, he knew that only Sunset, among the chestnuts, could vie with the sprinting powers of the mare, and therefore he nodded.

"I am content," said he.

"Good!" cried the trader. Then he called in English: "Sammy! Sammy! Get out Jester for me, will you?"

There was a bustle of many voices. The rumor spread instantly far and wide that a stupid Indian was about to be trimmed by the clever storekeeper, and in less time than it takes to tell, a hundred men and boys were gathered to watch the race, while Jester was brought out.

He looked fit enough to make a joke of the mare. He was of good Kentucky saddle stock, with a generous portion of the blood of the thoroughbred in his veins. High-headed, dancing, fiery-eyed, he fretted against the strong curb. The storekeeper swung his bulk into the saddle with a grunt.

"Are you ready?" he asked.

Thunder Moon had stripped off the saddle, and left the mare with only a lead rope around her neck. She needed nothing more for guidance, because she would answer the pressure of heel and knee as readily as a man will answer a spoken command.

"She has legs!" cried one of the spectators.

"She'll need eight legs like that to keep up with Jester!" answered one of the others, and there was a roar of laughter in response.

Then a tall Indian, robed to the eyes—a Crow—said maliciously to Thunder Moon:

"Young man, you will go home naked today. You are matched against the fastest horse that the palefaces can bring against you!"

Said Thunder Moon:

"Let the horses run the race. Afterwards, the men can do the talking."

It was an old saying among the Cheyennes, and it silenced the Crow and made him set his teeth with a sudden click.

"Very well!" called the starter, who had taken his post with a red handkerchief in his hand, ready to let it fall. "Get out of the way, all of you. Somebody get up there by the gates, and warn every one against coming through. We don't want this race upset. Let 'Sawbones' have her chance to run, if she don't fall down when she tries to turn!"

Thunder Moon could not understand any of these words, but he could understand the gestures, well enough, and, above all, he could understand the jeering laughter. And his heart grew harder and harder with the passing of every moment. They were very wise, these palefaces, or they would never have been able to make such very big medicine as these rifles, which killed from afar. But also, they were cunning, cruel, and hard of heart. He did not like their faces. He did not like their leering, jeering glances. And most of all, he detested in them their lack of dignity.

A sudden prayer went up from his heart that the mare might humble these brutal fellows in the very dust!

Chapter Twenty-five

"I am ready," said Thunder Moon to his opponent, and with a sidewise sweep of his eyes he studied the features of Jester. He knew horses as well as any man could know them. He had been raised with them. He had learned to judge the differences which existed between the Indian ponies and the tall chestnuts which had been brought from the Far Land by Big Hard Face; and he knew at the first glance that this Jester was indeed an admirable creature and capable of great speed. At the same time, he had seen The Minnow beat the others of her own race, those tall cousins of hers descended from the heroic horses of Big Hard Face; and he trusted implicitly in her lightness of foot. Even if she could not vie with Sunset in a five-minute gallop, still she was better than most of the others.

Let Jester do his best, then, for Thunder Moon would be prepared for him.

But, in the first place, he would throw away not a single chance.

For that reason, he threw off the buffalo robe and jerked off over his head the fine deerskin tunic. Now he sat upon the back of the mare, naked to the waist, his trousers belted tightly around him. One could see, for the first time, the little medicine bag which he wore suspended from a braided bit of horsehair that ran around his neck. It was the skin of a chipmunk, brought from a far section of the prairie, and it was stuffed with various things known only to Thunder Moon. In that medicine bag, he was convinced, his immortal soul was lodged.

Now that he was stripped to the waist, and ready to cut as little wind as possible, one might have thought that the men of the fort would have been amazed by the wonderful muscular strength which that back, and shoulders, and arched breast, and sinewy arms presented. But those frontiersmen were accustomed to seeing fellows of heroic proportions; and there was simply a grunt of admiration, and some surprise, that an Indian should be seen, with the muscular development which, generally speaking, belonged to the white man alone.

It was not, then, the heroic proportions of Thunder Moon that caught their eyes, nor the odd little medicine bag that swung from his neck; it was rather the color of the skin of this Cheyenne. It was a deep, glistening nut brown, every bit of it; but there was not the faintest tint of the copperish glow which distinguished the Indians from the white men. Any frontier lad, used to spending many an hour in the swimming pools, and well baked by the sun, could have showed you a body well-nigh as tanned as this.

"A funny looking Cheyenne, that one!" said someone.

"Half-breed," said another. "That's what he is."

"Not more than a quarter," said a third. "His face ain't made like a redskin's!"

It was not, as a matter of fact. The features were cleanly chiseled, a little too powerful and decided to be called handsome, but certainly cast after a most Caucasian mold. However, no one there even dreamed of the real truth—that there was not a drop of any but white man's blood in these veins. For, aside from little differences of features and color, in dress, in manner, in language, in headdress, and in the long black hair which flowed back over the shoulders and almost to the waist of Thunder Moon, he was typical Cheyenne. And when he heard English spoken, he turned upon the speakers an eye most convincingly blank.

"You watch yourself, Jeff Larned!" called one of his friends. "This here Cheyenne knows how to ride, and he ain't got such a bad horse. Cut the belly off of her, and she'd be a real speed machine."

"You leave her to Jester," said the storekeeper scornfully. "He's never been beat yet, you got to remember!"

This truth was enough to silence the doubter. The next moment the handkerchief fluttered down from the hand of the starter; and Thunder Moon, watching for the moment, tense, and quivering with an excitement which he had silently imparted to the good mare, shot away from the mark like an arrow from the vibrating string of a strong war bow.

She was a half jump ahead of Jester, though that horse had answered the signal like the uncoiling of a watch spring; and now, as they settled into full stride, Thunder Moon, glancing down, saw the shadow of the racing Jester diminishing rapidly beside him.

The Minnow, as she had often done before, was simply leaving her rival behind! Thunder Moon leaning down, whispered a word which she well knew. Gradually she abated her speed. Still her ears were flattened as though with the greatness of her effort, and still her head was stretched straight forth before her; but, nevertheless, her stride was less, and Jester began to pick up rapidly on his rival.

"You got the early speed!" shouted Jeff Larned, as he drew up even. "But now watch what happens to your clown of a horse!"

Thunder Moon did not understand these words, which had been spoken in English, but he could interpret the gesture and the tone, well enough.

However, he said nothing, and he brought the mare gently to the side of the gate and, touching the wall, turned her. Jester had already whipped about and was digging up a cloud of dust to get under full way, once more.

But what was a cloud of dust to a horse and a rider accustomed to riding into a mass of buffalo? Thunder Moon allowed himself one fierce, short laugh behind that cloud of dust, and then he flattened himself close to the neck of the mare and swung her forward into her full stride. Every swing of her stride was accompanied by a forward sway of his body.

Jester came smoothly, rhythmically back to them; and before them, Thunder Moon saw a wild confusion of waving arms and excited faces, and he heard a frenzy of noise. For it seemed as though the famous Jester was at last to be beaten. It was more than a seeming; for now, Thunder Moon sent the mare quickly past her rival and she went over the finish half a length to the good.

He jumped to the ground and strode through the excited mob to the front of the store. There he picked up the booty, sorted it, and laid aside five of the rifles which he did not want.

"How much powder and lead," he said, "for these guns?"

The storekeeper was in a frenzy of rage. It was true that he had been paid three times over for all the rifles of the first sale and those wagered in the bet; but he was in a black humor.

"Confound the rifles!" he roared. "Here—I'll change

'em for that much powder and that much of bullets all molded for you. That's fair enough!"

It was hardly a third of the value of the five extra rifles, in powder and in lead, but Thunder Moon thought it a handsome quantity. It was his first experience in conducting transactions with the whites. He was yet to learn of what trickery they were capable. And his eyes flashed with joy as he gathered in the bags of powder and lead. Surely his companions who waited in the prairie would be well pleased with all of this.

But there was a murmur through the crowd. They were used to seeing people cheated. They rather admired a clever tradesman; and they had no love, certainly, for the redskins. But, after all, those methods of Jeff Larned were a little too raw; and if the whole Cheyenne tribe were to learn how one of their members had been grossly cheated, might not the whole of that body of matchless warriors go on the war trail?

So the murmur swept through the mass, and Jeff Larned heard it, and grew more furious still. For he saw that he was losing not only a small portion of his dishonest profits, but a great deal of reputation as well.

He could not stand that.

"Friend, I shall let the same horse race against your mare, because I still think that he can beat her; and I'll double the stakes!" he cried.

"No," said Thunder Moon, for he was anxious to make off with his loot. "No, I have what I wish, and now I must go!"

He would have made off, but a great hand of steel gripped his shoulder and halted him.

He turned swiftly around, and there was a glint of danger in his eyes.

"Don't manhandle a redskin, Jeff, unless you're watching his knife hand!" warned a voice.

"Mind your business!" barked Jeff. "Cheyenne," he went on, "I'll tell you what I'll do. I'll wager you, two against one. You've got nine rifles, now, and you've got a tidy lot of powder and lead. I'll match Jester against the lot, and I'll match him against the mare, too! What do

you say? Do you hear me, young man? You go back to
your people rich and famous, or else you walk back with
nothing. You go back with your mare and with a picture
horse like Jester, or else you go back bare!"

Thunder Moon listened; and his soul was sorely tempted. For surely the mare had beaten the fast horse with
greater ease than this fellow could even guess. Yet somewhere there must be a trick, or the man would never
wager so confidently. He swiftly scanned all the possibilities of which he could think.

"What do you wager?" asked Thunder Moon reluc-
tantly. "I have what I wish, and I am ready to go back,
friend."

Jeff Larned was now in a white-hot passion. His judgment no longer cautioned him or even suggested some
sharper way of cheating the Indian again, as he had before. He knew simply that the mare had been able to beat
Jester by a scant half length; and he was positive that he
had up his sleeve a manner of defeating the mare by an
even greater distance. Therefore, what difference did it
make if he increased the offer?

He translated those rifles, and the powder and lead,
which he had lost, into their real values, and hastily he
piled together more guns.

"No more rifles," said Thunder Moon. "I have
enough!"

"How about this, then!"

Knives, and bags of powder, and quantities of bullets
were produced—enough ammunition for a regiment. The
heart of Thunder Moon ached with desire as he saw it all
heaped together. And still the storekeeper was putting
more on the heap. He brought out bright beads and colored cloths, until Thunder Moon with impassive face
stopped him again.

For, though beads and colored cloths might please the
Cheyennes, there was something in his soul which they
failed altogether to touch. Besides, of what use would all
of these trinkets be on the long march against the Comanches of the Southland? So thought Thunder Moon,
and denied the things with an impassive face.

But there was still a store from which he could be tempted. Revolvers were already worn freely, here and there, though old-fashioned men preferred pistols with one or two barrels. And now Jeff Larned jerked out a half dozen of the new weapons and scattered them on the porch, with a quantity of ammunition for them.

"There, Cheyenne!" said the storekeeper. "Put your eye on those!"

Thunder Moon picked up one of the guns. He had not the slightest idea that he had come to one of the important crossways of his life. He examined it and the oiled and easy mechanism with wonder.

"Is it a small rifle?" he asked.

"Rifle?" scoffed the excited Larned. "It's six rifles boiled down small—at short range!"

"Is it really not a toy?" asked Thunder Moon, still more rapt.

"Toy, eh? Look at this!" And Larned snatched one of the weapons from his hip pocket and opened fire.

It was beyond credence.

Across the street there was a gaudy sign which proclaimed that the blacksmith shop of Hal Green was the best one west of the Mississippi. Six times, as fast as one could count, the little gun spoke from the hip of Larned; and six neat round holes were punched at the center of the sign across the street.

The cloud of smoke blew away. Even the rough men of Fort Humphrey Brown had been impressed. Thunder Moon was plainly awed.

"Will these others make the same medicine?" he asked breathlessly.

"Aye, aye!" exclaimed Mr. Larned. "With the triggers out you can shoot 'em all with the thumb. 'Fan' is the word for it."

"It is enough!" said Thunder Moon, and he half closed his eyes. For he saw a startling vision of a battle charge of the Cheyenne tribe, with himself in the lead. He saw the lines close on Pawnee enemies. He saw the rifles discharged, and the warriors sweeping on through, while from his hands, two little weapons were spitting forth a fiery rain of death!

Better than rifle, bow, or knife were these treasures!

"Make them so that they are all like that one," said Thunder Moon, pointing to the still smoking weapon in the hand of Jeff Larned, "and we run the race again!"

Chapter Twenty-six

The time was to come when red men and white would curse the name of Jeff Larned, who placed these new and dreadful weapons in the hands of Thunder Moon; but that time was still in the future.

As the spectators saw the storekeeper feverishly preparing the revolvers to meet the demand of the Cheyenne, they murmured, one to the other, that Larned for the first time in history was actually offering money's worth. But what was the trick up the sleeve of this shrewd trader? What made him so sure that he would win the race, after being fairly beaten once? Certainly it could not be that he thought the mare was exhausted by her first effort. Not a hair of her coat had turned, and her eye was as bright as ever, as she stood back of her master.

Jeff Larned's two hired men were working rapidly, now, taking down the Colts, filing out the trigger mechanism inside, and assembling them again; but this time, and while the pause endured, the word went out, and more and more men gathered—soldiers and citizens, children and women, to stare at the sweating shopkeeper, long famous for his strength of hand and quickness of wit, and to stare, too, at the Indian's mare, and at the tall Indian himself, wrapped again in his buffalo robe, and impassive of face.

A smooth-faced young sprig of a lieutenant with a soft Southern drawl remarked: "No wonder that she beat Larned's horse. She'll beat him again, most likely. She's a queer-looking one—but thoroughbred, every inch of her! I'd like to know whose scalp was lifted before she passed into Cheyenne hands! What's the record of this buck?"

No one knew. They had never seen this brave before. But they could be sure, though they knew it not, that they would see him again.

"It's finished," said Jeff Larned, bringing the guns out again. "Here's a loaded revolver for you, Cheyenne. It'll speak with six tongues for you, just the same as it did for me. You raise the hammer with the thumb of your hand; you aim by pointing; and you fire."

The gun was taken. The crowd scattered back. The Colt exploded, and by the grace of purest accident, another round hole appeared in the sign of the blacksmith across the street. Thunder Moon could not help a grave exclamation. He saw himself raised at a stroke to the eminent rank of the most feared and famous brave among the Cheyennes.

"Are you ready again?" asked Thunder Moon.

"One minute," said the storekeeper. "The horse is ready. Hey, Sammy! Come here!"

A withered youngster of fifteen came hastily forward, grinning with a guilty self-consciousness of the part which he was about to play. He was thrown up into the saddle by Larned, and the latter stepped back with a broader grin than had yet appeared on his face, that day.

"Now, Cheyenne," said he, "we're ready for the second race!"

"Hello, Larned! That's a raw trick!" exclaimed the young lieutenant from the South, who was new on the border and still new to its ways and its men.

"Leave me and my tricks be!" exclaimed Larned. "I told him that I'd race Jester against his mare, again. I didn't say that I'd be in the saddle once more! Cheyenne, you ride, or you give up your loot, and the mare that goes with it!"

And as he spoke, he was fortified by a grim chuckle from the crowd. Certainly this was sharp practice, but it was sharp practice at the expense of an Indian, and among the frontiersmen, the red man was looked upon as a sort of hybrid species—a little above the snake and a good deal below the wolf.

An ounce of lead through the brain was the best medicine for any redskin was the universal belief along the border. Thunder Moon, looking helplessly around the circle, felt that there would be no champions for his cause. And if he attempted to resist the wiles of this brutal white man—he already saw the strong hand of the latter gripping the little revolver in his hip pocket! That would settle all arguments with one swift word. The rifle of Thunder Moon was far away with his saddle, on the ground; so, gloomily, he swung onto the back of the mare. He had little hope of winning. Even The Minnow, strong and swift as she was, could hardly give a hundred pounds to such a horse as Jester and win from him!

But he turned her head toward the gates, and in his heart, there swelled the first wave of profound, black hatred of the white man, and all of his ways. Scalps? Yes, he would take them willingly, if they could come from the heads of white men!

"It'll teach the Cheyennes that here in Fort Brown we've got brains," chuckled Jeff Larned. "Hey, clear the path! Get the race started!"

In an instant all was ready; the handkerchief dropped and away went the mare as before. Once more she gained the advantage at the start, but even more decisively, this time. She was a full length away, before the weak hands of the boy rider could urge Jester to full speed; and she increased that advantage, whipping instantly into full stride. With every trick of the rider's trade, Thunder Moon urged her forward toward the gates.

But now it was a different story; for there on the ground beside him, the shadow of Jester's head was creeping evenly and smoothly up with him. That handsome head gained, reached his side, the shoulder of the mare—and here were the gates!

Swinging the mare with a touch of his knee, Thunder Moon hurled his whole weight to the inside of the half circle in which she turned—threw himself with a jerk, and catching the ridge of her back with an expert heel; and the clever trick snapped her around like the lash of a whip. She was away toward the goal once more, with Thunder Moon slipping back into his place and driving her forward with rapid, eager words at her ear, for he had actual hope of winning, now. The turn had cost Jester two lengths. He was laboring hard as he straightened for the finish. But could he make up the distance in this short stretch?

There at the finish, men were frozen to silence by the greatness of their excitement; and Thunder Moon saw Jeff Larned standing half crouched, with arms held forward, like one about to leap into a death grapple.

Behind Thunder Moon came the shadow of the Jester. At every stride the beautiful gelding gained with a terrible certainty. But the line drew nearer. Past Thunder Moon went Jester's head, past the shoulder of The Minnow, and then along her neck. As they came head and head, the line was crossed!

Who had won? One clearly ringing voice proclaimed the truth:

"The Indian collects on this race!"

It was the young lieutenant from the South.

Chapter Twenty-seven

In the wild confusion of voices that followed Thunder Moon as he went across the line, he distinguished the tall Indian who had been looking on before. Now, as Thunder Moon drew up The Minnow, while Jester flashed on ahead, this Indian said calmly but sharply:

"You have won, Cheyenne. But you will never take the prize home with you! Here are too many little guns and big ones!"

Thunder Moon turned anxiously back toward the start, and there he came upon the burly form of Jeff Larned heaping together all of the loot for which the race had been run.

"Take it back!" he was saying to his assistants. "This here was a dead heat. It was a draw. Nobody won the race, and it's got to be run over again!"

He turned to Thunder Moon and repeated those words harshly in Sioux, but the latter shook his head. By trickery and the most clever riding, and by taking advantage of every chance of the race, he had managed to bring The Minnow home a winner, the first time, but he knew perfectly well that he would not be able to succeed a second time. He had won. Therefore there was no need of a second running.

So he said, gravely and slowly, remembering the manner of Lame Eagle in a crisis. For that great chieftain always floated before the eyes of Thunder Moon as an ideal, often unattainable but always to be imitated as closely as possible. So now, while the hot blood surged up and set his temples aching with the violence of its pulsation, he controlled himself with a severe effort. The voice of Lame Eagle had never been known to grow sharp or high or overloud except when he cheered on wavering warriors to the battle charge.

"I have won," said Thunder Moon. "It was said by the men who stood at the finish. I have won. Why should I race again?"

"Who says that you won?" roared Jeff Larned, glaring around him, and with his right hand gripping the revolver in his hip pocket again.

His glance roved over many a brave face and many a stern one, passing across that crowd, but there was not one who cared to stand up for his convictions against this known man-killer and expert duelist. Only one slender youth, quietly, almost carelessly, answered:

"I was standing exactly at the finish line. I know that the mare had her nose, and more, in front as she went across!"

"*You* know!" yelled Larned, lashing himself easily into a fury. "*You* know! And who might you be? And who made you a judge? And if you made yourself the boss here, I'll unmake you!"

Thunder Moon looked in bewilderment at the young, dark-faced fellow. The words he could not understand, but the manner was unmistakable. Here was a man who was maintaining the right of The Minnow in this hostile atmosphere—a man he had never seen before and might never see again.

It was very strange. Perhaps even among the palefaces there were a few equipped with the indomitable nobility of Lame Eagle. For now the slip of a lieutenant was saying:

"Larned, you must not speak to me or any other man in this fashion. It won't do!"

"You say it won't do!" raged Larned. "I say that it will do. It's got to do. I'm here to make it do! You and your family behind you are a bunch of swine and hounds. I'm telling you that!"

"I'll give you while I count to ten," said the youth, "to unsay that, Larned!"

"Ten? Not while you count a hundred!"

Thunder Moon needed no explanation. There was to be a fight. The form of the soldier had become stiff and straight. His face was gray. But he did not falter. Plainly, he knew that he had no chance against the trained gun of the storekeeper, but still he would not flinch from his duty.

However, even a white man must not fight the quarrels of Thunder Moon.

One long, gliding step placed him between the two.

"Speak to me," said he.

He had folded his arms, and perhaps that was what tempted Larned to use his hands instead of his gun. Besides, his hands were his favorite weapons. Guns and knives were delightful, to be sure; but there was infinitely more satisfaction in laying a man low with a pile-driver punch, and then grappling him, and breaking him.

He smote from the hip up, leaving the gun behind. But his punch clove the air. Thunder Moon had wavered back just the proper distance to escape a blow attempted without warning, and before the other fist of the storekeeper could be whipped across to the head, Thunder Moon was in close and fixing his grip.

He had wrestled all his life, with the sturdy Indian lads of the Cheyenne village. He had learned lightning speed from them, but he had a natural power of hand and arm which no Cheyenne could ever have possessed.

Now, under his fingers, he felt such swelling, surging muscles as he never touched before. However, a wrench, a twist—and the storekeeper fell with a crash. He gasped, more stunned in fallen dignity than hurt in body. Then he writhed for a new hold, but a cold bit of steel was pressed beneath his chin. His own revolver had been snatched from his hip pocket, and it was with this that Thunder Moon threatened him, holding the hammer back with his thumb.

"Help!" yelled Jeff Larned, seeing Providence unwelcomely close to him. "He's goin' to murder me!"

But no one stirred. Revolvers are not to be tampered with. Besides, this was the bully of the fort, and it was time that he had his lesson, no matter how he had to pay for it. And the Indian was saying gravely:

"You wear the first scalp that I have ever wanted to take. Thank your good fortune that you are not alone with me on the prairie. Now lie here like the dog that you are. Move a hand, and I kill you!"

He rose and stepped back, and the trader lay deathly still. He still had his knife, but in the hand of his enemy was the revolver, and he had seen that the instinct for revolver play was in this strange Indian youth.

Thunder Moon, stepping back, shoved the revolver inside the belt which held up his trousers. And with half an eye upon the prostrate form of Jeff Larned, he loaded all his winnings upon the backs of Jester and of The Minnow. All the heavy bags of powder and of leaden bullets, and all the strong rifles, and above all those beautiful little new weapons, he packed together.

Last of all, he leaped upon the back of The Minnow.

"Lie still, dog of a white man," said he. "I have not seen you for the last time. I go on a long journey, but I shall return. Your scalp is loose on your head. I shall take it. The Sky People hear me promise. It shall dry in the tepee of Big Hard Face."

He swept his eye over the crowd. He picked out the face of the lieutenant, and extending his muscular arm, he grasped the lad's hand. He knew only one word of the white man's tongue, but he said it now with his heart in his voice: "Friend!"

"Friend!" repeated the lieutenant, much moved. Then Thunder Moon sent the mare ahead, and, still turned back, covered the trader's body with his rifle.

At length, he was at a safe distance, and turning about in the saddle, he jerked the lead rope to bring Jester into a gallop, and so swept through the gate and out onto the level ground beyond.

Behind him, he heard one frantic yell of rage and despair from Jeff Larned as that worthy leaped to his feet at last. But the victory remained with Thunder Moon. He had the horse and the loot of the storekeeper. There was nothing on four feet within the fort fast enough to attempt a pursuit of him. So, utterly secure, as though an ocean lay between him and his recent enemy, he gave The Minnow her head, knowing that she would steer straight back to the spot where she had last parted from the rest of the horses. And The Minnow went, straight as an arrow.

In the meantime, his thoughts were dwelling on the strength of Fort Humphrey Brown. And vague plans formed in his brain. War was a great vocation. He loved it with all of his heart. Twice and again, he had burst through the lines of Pawnees. Twice, also, in the open battlefield, he had charged the Blackfeet home. There was a small spot under his right shoulder, silver-white, where a Blackfoot lance had sunk deep in his body. And there were other minor cuts and bruises to remember. Nevertheless, war was inexpressibly sweet.

But war against the might and the cunning of the white man? War against his thunder guns and his many new devices? That would be a thing to test nerves of steel, and on the spot, he vowed that one day he would grow great enough to gather the Cheyennes behind him, and with the warriors armed with fine rifles, and trained in the use of them, he would storm Fort Humphrey Brown. He would pass through those brutal, savage, sneering, cynical white men. He would leave them lying in their own blood. Their scalps should be tied to the spearheads of the noble Cheyennes. And that victory would give the tribe the looting of the lordly place!

What loot! What incalculable riches to be taken home! And with the might thus added, to turn from side to side, and send the Pawnees and the Blackfeet reeling back from their established ranges, and afterward, to crush even the lordly Sioux, and in their desert fastnesses, to teach the Comanches that they had masters.

The beautiful dream of conquest unfolded like a flower in the brain of Thunder Moon. He had seen hostile Indian powers, before this. But none had so irritated and thrilled him as had this visit to the whites. He raised his hands palms up to the heavens, and there he saw his familiar cloud of shining white floating in the heart of the sky. It was like a supernatural promise, to Thunder Moon, that the Sky People would help him to the great things for which he hoped!

Chapter Twenty-eight

These great aspirations, which now first entered the brain of Thunder Moon, and which were afterward to involve him and others in so much trouble, so completely occupied him that when he returned to his companions, their wonder and joy at seeing the rifles and the loads of ammunition, and the fine new horse, Jester, and even their ecstasy when he demonstrated the possibilities of the little revolvers to them, hardly moved him. They were like things that pass in a dream; for in his imagination he was still taking scalps and plundering cities, and he felt himself lifted above the world which he had known before.

He had found an enemy truly worthy of his steel, and he
rejoiced in the discovery. He had taken the one great step
which passes a youth into full manhood.

His companions felt the difference and thought that it
was because they were now viewing him with a newer and
intenser vision because of his great feat. Their eyes had
been opened by this achievement of his in entering the
fort and returning with such unhoped-for treasures. Now
and again, hardy and daring youngsters as they were,
their minds were sometimes overawed by the tremendous
venture to which they had committed themselves so carelessly; and as the days and weeks found them farther and
farther west and south, they took thought and often
wished themselves back with their fellow tribesmen; but
on such occasions, the unshaken calmness and gravity of
their leader reassured them. He had, in fact achieved a
greater victory over his fellows than over Jeff Larned. For
this stroke of business gave them the utmost confidence in
their leader; knowing him brave and successful in battle,
they now felt that he was the complete man, incapable of
serious mistakes. He had hypnotized them perfectly by his
stroke in the fort. It made no difference that Snake-that-
talks or some of the others had to point out the way
across the prairies. It made no difference that Big River,
or one of the other keen hunters, was always the first to
solve the trail problems when they were in the pursuit of
difficult game. The deficiencies of Thunder Moon were
not noted by his followers. They served him with a blind
devotion, always feeling that he was the brain and they
the mere hands of this enterprise. And the time came
when a word of praise from Thunder Moon was as much
to one of the others as a scalp taken or a *coup* counted.

Perhaps it would be best to think of these voyagers of
the prairie as of people embarked in a ship, crossing a
vast ocean under slow and uncertain sail, compelled to
digress from the course from time to time, by the necessity of hunting food, and delayed by mishaps to the craft
which must be repaired.

In the meantime, like a good ship's captain, Thunder
Moon constantly exercised his crew at their arms. They

were going against desperate warriors, and therefore he had them work with lance and shield every day, and the war hatchets were flung, and the war bows were aimed constantly at targets until his heroes were perfected in the art of war. Thunder Moon's heart swelled with pride at their skill.

But most of all, he kept them working with the rifles. He knew that there were two great faults with Indian marksmen: that they were more apt to worship a gun than to practice with it, and that they were not likely to keep the weapon in good condition. In the old days of his clumsy and backward boyhood, when he despaired of ever equaling the other youngsters with bow, or knife, or club, or ax, he had devoted himself with all his mind to the rifle, where skill counted more than strength, and he had mastered all of its arts with the patience of an Indian, and the craft of a white man. And now he taught his braves every detail of their weapons, how to make them apart and reassemble them, and how to oil, and grease, and clean them. More than this, they had a constant drill in pointing the long guns, and a certain amount of powder was burned and lead spent each day in actual shooting. And, at length, he felt that every one of the five far surpassed the most practiced warriors left behind in the tribe. But there was another result; for as they felt their skill increasing, their confidence in their teacher-leader and in their own prowess grew limitless. They would have followed him into a whole host of enemies!

There were troubles, of course. The greatest of all occurred early in the trip, when three of the revolvers which he had intrusted to his friends were hopelessly ruined, and Young Hawk was badly burned and his hand lamed for a week on account of a misfire and explosion.

After that Thunder Moon realized that these instruments were too delicate and precise for the uneducated hands of his friends. He kept them for himself, and made three holsters, after the fashion in which he had seen the men at the fort wear the guns. Two, he tied to the saddle, one he wore at his hip; and they were rarely out of his hands. He worked with a ceaseless patience to acquire the skill that Jeff Larned had exhibited in snatching the heavy Colt from his pocket faster than the very thought of another man could work. And he learned, like Jeff Larned, to shoot from the hip, firing with the hammer of the gun, and dispensing altogether with the trigger.

He showed what his skill amounted to more than once on that inland voyage, but particularly on a day when the party, with Yellow Wolf in the lead, came up a dry canyon against a severe wind and, turning an elbow of the cliff, ran onto a big grizzly which reared from the carcass of a dead buffalo which it had been devouring.

Yellow Wolf made his horse leap to the side, and he shrieked with surprise and terror as the monster lurched down on all fours and charged. Thunder Moon came next in line and he did not move Sunset from his place. There was not time to draw the long rifle from its case beneath his right leg, but he caught the little Colt in his hand, and six explosions followed faster than a rapid tongue could count.

The grizzly whirled and dropped dead, and when they examined it, they found that the whole front of its face had been destroyed by the deadly shower of lead, while one slug had passed through the eye, and so into the brain. It made a great difference to Thunder Moon to learn exactly what the Colt could accomplish, but it was not a matter of skill in the eyes of his companions. The thing had been done so swiftly and perfectly that it seemed to them a case of very big Medicine; it was as though this leader of theirs had snatched a six-forked thunderbolt from heaven and cast it at the lumbering brute.

From the claws, a necklace was made, and Thunder Moon, you may be sure, was mightily pleased to wear it; for the trophies of a grizzly, killed in single fight, were as honorable as a scalp taken in war.

Hundreds of leagues now lay behind them. Thunder Moon was now sun-darkened almost to the shade of his companions. All the party was lean and fit from much riding and constant exercise with their arms, from many a terrific, but friendly, wrestling bout in the cool of the evening, and from many a foot race over the prairies. Thunder Moon himself, to set the example and keep them all in perfect fitness, would often drop from the saddle and jog mile after mile across the prairie with the horse following him; for he was trying to live up to all of the good traditions of the warpath which he had heard from his father and Lame Eagle.

So they crossed the very edge of the territory of the gigantic Osages, at last, and crossed the waters of the mighty Arkansas, and found themselves in the land of the Comanches! From that moment, what had been caution before became scrupulous care. They lived on water and dried meat; or, when cooking must be done, it was accomplished at night, when the smoke would not show, and over a hooded fire, so that not so much as a single red eye of light might look forth across the desert and warn the enemy.

It was a new land, moreover. Even the cunning of Snake-that-talks was severely tested by the ceaseless deserts. There were long marches without water, and the water they found often consisted merely of half-dried, filthy pools, with scum around the edges. There were no buffalo. Game was dreadfully scarce. And the most expert marksmanship was required to knock over the lightning-footed jack rabbits, or the sand-colored antelope which darted across the sky line like low-winging birds. If they needed a razor edge put on their marksmanship it was accomplished now.

They went on slowly, feeling their way, always with one of the party far ahead to the right and another in a similar position to the left, like the antennae of a creeping insect, ready to report trouble ahead. But the chief reason for their slowness was that Thunder Moon refused to work his horses to skin and bone. He saw that they worked themselves as hard as the men, but when leanness became exaggerated, there was a resolute halt in some favorable spot until they had recuperated their strength. For the time might be, he knew, when all their strength and speed of foot might be needed if this war party was to return without loss to the home lodges. And the day was to come when all would bless him for the caution which irked them so often on the march.

It was the constant hope of Thunder Moon that his vigilance would bring him up to a Comanche village by surprise in the middle of night, and then they could work such exploits as would cover them with fame and steal back undiscovered, but fortune checked him rudely. Yellow Wolf, scouting in the bright heat of a morning, waved from a distance the sign of "Enemies" and "Comanches." They were hardly under way, when they saw behind them a dozen riders streaking across the prairie after them; and as they rode, the sun glinted in long rays along the barrels of their rifles. A dozen Comanches, then, and all well-armed! But such was the spirit in the band which followed Thunder Moon that they would have turned at once and charged the enemy home!

"Listen to me, brothers," said he. "We have heard much about the winged horses of the Comanches. Let us test their speed, first. And afterward, I promise you shall see fighting enough!"

Chapter Twenty-nine

They swung away, five swift riders on perfect horses, and gathering in their left-hand scout, Big River, as they went, they loosed their mounts to full speed.

There was no need to do so for long. In ten minutes, the Comanches were dwindling fast behind them, and Thunder Moon sat back in his saddle and brought Sunset to a hand gallop. But the others were openly exultant.

"Are these the terrible Comanches and their matchless horses?" shouted Standing Bear. "I tell you, they are the blackbirds, and we are hawks. We can fly around them and kill them one by one and laugh at them. We could fly away from a hundred thousand of such riders!"

"Slowly! Slowly!" said Thunder Moon. "No man is

dead till his scalp is tied to the lance head. Now ride carefully, but not too carefully. Let it seem that our horses are merely tiring from the race!"

So it was done, and the Comanches swept rapidly up from the rear and drew out of the cloud of their dust. Twelve half-naked braves, they loomed up, each riding with a desperate abandon, and each brandishing his rifle as though he were already counting on the scalps which he would take.

"They have us in their hands, they think," said Thunder Moon to Yellow Wolf. "Look, brother! And listen, also. They scream like hungry wolves! Well, one of them, at least, will be no longer hungry before the sun sets!" And he shook his rifle as he spoke. "Now listen to what I say, all of you. Ride as if in fear of your lives. Bend low, pretend to flog your horses, but all the time hold them in. Look back, often, as if you feared the death which was coming to you. But when I shout, then each man turn his horse, top him, and take quick aim and fire. Then charge them, as I shall show you how to do! Do you hear?"

They heard. And instantly, delighted in the stratagem, as though the grim odds of two to one were nothing to them, they bent over the necks of their steeds, and pretended to urge them forward, still glancing over their shoulders as though in terror.

In the meantime, Thunder Moon was carefully calculating the distance. He saw the Comanches hurl up behind them, growing larger, and coming into point-blank range, but still, like men sure of their game, they would not fire at the fugitives, reserving their shots for still closer execution. They swept nearer and nearer, riding like demigods rather than men, and their screeching war yells tore the ears of Thunder Moon. He was, in fact, more than half afraid. But all the while he measured distances, and then a shout of savage delight ripped from his throat. That instant, each of the flying chestnuts planted its feet, halted in a sliding shower of sand and dirt, and whirled about; and the fugitive Cheyennes, sitting calm and erect in the saddle, leveled their rifles, aimed, and fired.

The Comanches, conscious at last that there had been some trickery, wavered for an instant, but conscious of their superior strength in numbers, they bore straight in. Two or three of their own guns exploded, but they were random shots fired from galloping horses; and then the blast of musketry was driven into their faces.

Thunder Moon saw his chosen target drop from the saddle. Another horse galloped riderless over the plains, and a third scoured off with a half-helpless rider sagging on his back.

Still those were dauntless Comanches, and their numbers were fifty per cent greater than those of their enemies in spite of this loss. They rushed on, yelling wildly, firing first with their rifles as they came, and then with arrows strung upon their war bows. Thunder Moon had given the word, and he himself was the cutting edge of the wedge of Cheyennes that darted to meet the enemy. His men behind him rode fast and well, their arrows hissing through the air, but they could not keep pace with the gigantic strides of Sunset.

It seemed that Thunder Moon had thrown himself into the very hands of the foes and a groan went up from his brothers-in-arms. But as for him, never had such a surge of confident joy beat in any human breast. With heel and knee he held Sunset steady beneath him, and in either hand he carried a shining little weapon, each loaded with flashing death.

He saw before him the dusty, seated forms of the Comanches. He saw the flashing of their teeth as they yelled in furious exultation; and, then, as an arrow hummed past his head and as the flash of a gun was just before him, he opened fire!

That ended the battle, as surely as though the heavens had opened and poured down lightning. A feathered chief before him threw wide his arms and sailed sidewise from the saddle, dead. To right and left the guns spat ruin among the wild riders.

A wail of terror and woe rose from the stricken warriors. It was not battle. It was mystery—it was the hand of the gods—it was the working of a dreadfully great Medicine!

Thunder Moon swung Sunset around with a desperate eagerness, as soon as he could check the impetus of that forward charge; for he had still bullets in each revolver, and a third gun in reserve, but he saw that the work was done.

Of the nine Comanches who had met the charge, five were actually down, and the remaining four fled as though from certain death, clinging to their horses, too terrified to so much as turn and launch arrows at their pursuers. And Sunset was instantly away in the van of pursuit bound on the traces of the most splendid rider of the fugitives.

But if flight with the intention of turning to battle had been pleasant, how pleasant, how wonderfully sweet was pursuit now. Now, Comanches, let the boasted speed of the desert horses be proved! And proved they were; for long-striding, dauntless in courage, fleeter than antelope though they were, behind them came horses of a greater race, longer-legged, longer-striding, swifter of foot. And they ran up on the Comanches like greyhounds upon mastiffs.

The war yell parted the lips of Thunder Moon. He saw the warrior before him wheel in the saddle with desperately contorted face to launch a shaft; straight into that contorted face the bullet sped, and the brave fell back over the tail of his horse and rolled in a shapeless heap upon the prairie. But still the bloodthirst was not satisfied, and Thunder Moon swung the stallion about to seek another prey.

Behold, there was not one left!

Of the remaining three, two were already down, and he was just in time to see the lance of Big River thrust through the body of the last survivor. Now, only the savage and joyous yells of the Cheyennes rang across the plain! So he himself turned back, hotly, furiously. Let him work while the madness was still upon him, and rip the scalp from the head of his last victim. Had he not promised scalps to Big Hard Face?

He leaped from Sunset, knife in hand, in time to see a fallen Comanche, in the distance, rise again, and try to pick up a rifle—in time, also, to see Yellow Wolf drag back the foeman by the hair, and plunge a knife in his throat.

Thunder Moon grew dizzy and half sick. But he knelt quickly upon the shoulders of his fallen Indian, gripped the scalp lock, and set the knife against the taut skin.

There was a faint groan, and the knife dropped from the hand of Thunder Moon. He whipped it up again, furious at his own womanish weakness, but his fingers that had been iron in battle were nerveless, now. And turning the victim upon his back, he saw that the bullet had glanced along the cheek bone and up the side of the head of the Comanche. It was a long and bleeding wound, but not really serious.

That moment, the brave recovered complete consciousness. He started up, writhing to get free, and Thunder Moon suddenly sprang back, rejoicing. "Draw your knife, Comanche!" he challenged. "I throw my gun away. I stand to meet you, man to man."

"Good!" said the other. His rolling eyes took in the slaughter of his companions; and then he charged to avenge their deaths. But his step was staggering, his knife stroke wild, and Thunder Moon, dropping his weapon, caught the other in his naked hands and mastered him swiftly and easily, for the bullet had stolen the strength of the big Indian.

A twist of leather thong around his wrists, and the capture was made, and the *coup* had been counted. Another around his feet, and Thunder Moon could leave his prisoner and go back to the main scene of the battle, where his companions were now holding mad carnival. Two scalps hung from the lance of Yellow Wolf, and Big River, streaked with blood, carried two also. Each of the rest had taken a single trophy, but three dead men lay on the plain, untouched, and Thunder Moon marveled. Never before had he seen or heard of redmen holding back from snatching scalps with a jealous hand; but the three braves who had fallen before his rifle and his revolver shots had not been disturbed as they lay. Their scalps were left for him and he grew sick and giddy again at the thought!

One by one he went to the prostrate forms. Each of them he touched. And with each touch he pronounced the formula: "I, Thunder Moon, count this *coup* on the Comanches!"

But then he turned slowly toward the others, and the words came of their own accord: "Snake-that-talks, Standing Bear, and Young Hawk, each of you has only one scalp. Why is that? There are three waiting for you!"

"Look, brother," said Snake-that-talks, moved by this unheard-of generosity, "there is not yet one scalp in your tepee of your taking. Will you let this harvest go?"

"The Comanches are a standing field of grain," said Thunder Moon faintly. "They wait for me to come to them, and there are other days when I shall find them. And look yonder, brothers! One of the dogs has escaped from us! He will go to spread the word that we are among his people, like wolves among calves. Yellow Wolf and Big River, take your horses, and ride, ride to take him! Or he will open the eyes of all his nation about us!"

And he pointed far off where, through the crystal-clear air of the plain, the form of the Comanche who had been stunned in the first discharge of firearms was now scarcely visible, wavering against the far horizon.

Chapter Thirty

A very stirring debate arose at once as to the best manner of torturing the prisoner to death, with the hope that he might reveal to them something valuable concerning his people—something by which they could profit to attack the Comanches with a greater advantage.

Thunder Moon, in the meantime, had washed the

wound along the head of his victim, and tied it with a bit of cotton cloth.

"Is all well with you, brother?" he asked, stepping back from his work.

He would never forget the strange look in the eyes of the Comanche as he looked up to the boyish face of his captor. It was a look of curiosity and surprise mingled with a stern certainty and a resolve like iron. It meant that he expected death, and death with all the devilish cruelties which Indian skill could make attend upon it.

"We have considered, O Thunder Moon," said Snake-that-talks, coming up with his eyes fixed steadily upon the Comanche. "And if you approve of it, we intend to tie him to that dead horse, and then shoot arrows into him— not through the head or heart, but little by little, sticking him full of iron, so that he will taste his death slowly. He is a man who has given death to many. Of those five scalps of which he can boast, how many were taken from the heads of the Cheyennes he met in battle and turned their souls into breaths of wind, dissolved forever!"

Thunder Moon regarded his captive again. He was ashamed of the inattentiveness which had kept him from seeing the outward signs that this was a man of mark among his people. But, indeed, Thunder Moon had long been famous among the Cheyennes for his blindness. Though he could look into the eyes of a man and read his soul better than all saving Lame Eagle, yet the exterior features were often completely missed by him.

And, glancing into the face of the warrior again, he said suddenly: "Who wore the scalps you have taken, my friend? And what is your name?"

"My name," said the captive readily enough, "is Walking Crow. There are Cheyennes who have heard it in battle! And of the scalps which I have taken, four are the souls of Cheyenne warriors."

A harsh exclamation of rage leaped from the mouth of Snake-that-talks, and he seemed about to leap at the throat of the Comanche; but a single glance from Thunder Moon checked him, and the prisoner vaunted savagely:

"Thunder Moon is a great chief. The Sky People listen to his voice. We have heard his name and know him. We have met him this day, and never before have the Cheyennes done such a deed as this. But I, Walking Crow, have been a great warrior, also. Now my soul is to blow away into dust. But I laugh. I cannot be sad. Tarawa has given me many glories, and though I perish forever and my scalp dries in the tepee of the great chief, Thunder Moon, still my people will never forget my name. It will live in the hearts of the Comanches, long after the Comanche spears have found your hearts!"

So said Walking Crow, like a brave Indian defying his enemies. But Thunder Moon was not enraged like his companions. "This man shall die tomorrow," said he. "There is no time to kill him now, slowly, as he deserves. Because, see! Our two brothers are returning to us!"

In fact, the two scouts were hurrying back toward them, and arrived with their chestnuts darkened with sweat and shining in the sun. They reported briefly that as they hurried after the wounded fugitive, they had seen, from a low knoll, the peaked tops of Comanche lodges in the far distance, but too close for them to get to the wounded man before he reached the town. So they hurried back with the word, and it was plain that these twelve warriors had but newly started on the warpath. They had barely left the sight of their city, when they encountered a more dreadful enemy than they had expected.

There was no more talk of torturing Walking Crow to death on the spot. But they gathered their spoil of beaded deerskin suits, and robes, and saddles, and horses, and spears, and shields, and above all the medicine bags and the scalps of the horsemen. Then they turned back, with Thunder Moon leading, and Snake-that-talks beside him. They turned back slowly, riding fresh horses, so that the ones they had raced to and fro in the battle could rest from their exertions. And as they rode, with the prisoner lashed on the back of Jester, Thunder Moon listened to the murmurs of talk behind him.

All that he heard was very sweet to him. For his followers were literally overwhelmed with awe at the work which they had accomplished under his leadership.

They had received not so much as a single scratch, so swiftly and completely had the chattering revolvers of Thunder Moon turned the Comanche charge into a hopeless rout. Under the broad shield of his wisdom and his courage, they had gained ten scalps, and a prisoner, too; and one wounded, wretched fugitive had barely managed to escape from the field and carry the alarm to the city of their enemies.

It was such a deed as might make even the heart of Lame Eagle swell with envy and wonder, and among the murmurs behind Thunder Moon were those which spoke of the days to come, when he should be the war chief of his people! He smiled faintly as he listened. When that day came, he would show them such wars as they had never dreamed of before; and, above all, his first blow would level the brutal men of Fort Humphrey Brown to the earth! But at one thing he wondered. While he was revolving in his mind the next stroke which he might strike for glory at the Comanches, his companions were eager for one thing only, and that was a return along the distant trail which led to their homes. They had done enough. They had bearded the lion in his den. They were anxious to go back and reap the harvest of praise!

But he himself was not content, and when the dusk gathered, and they could not see any sign of pursuit along the plain behind them, he turned his party to the side and led them toward the purple sunset hills to the north. There was no question as to his purpose; but when, as the evening darkened, he turned straight back under the shadow of the hills toward the encampment of the Comanches, the faces of his men were gloomy indeed!

However, it seemed to him that his course was as clear as day. Had he not proved that the Sky People were watching and helping him on this day? Therefore he would take advantage of good fortune, and profit by it while the tide of his luck was in.

So thought Thunder Moon, and he held steadily back on his course, keeping his horse to a smart pace, until, from the shoulder of a low eminence, he could look across the desert and see the scattered lights of the distant Comanche city. Through it ran the bright arc of a little river that extended from the hills through which they had been riding.

Then he gathered his men about him. He told them to cast lots to determine which of them should remain behind to guard the prisoner and to guard the plunder and most of the horses, while he and the rest slipped forward toward the town, to see what feat of arms could be accomplished. The lots were cast in silence. The choice fell upon Standing Bear; the others changed horses again, tightened their belts, and prepared to ride behind their leader. Only Yellow Wolf, more tried than all the others in former wars, ventured to say:

"It is a great city, brother. Their ways are strange to us. They could swallow us as a bear swallows a mouse!"

"Trust me," said Thunder Moon. "Have I not told you that I shall not go back to my people without a scalp? Therefore I know that something great still remains to be done. Perhaps the battle we have already won is nothing compared to the battle which we are now to fight!"

After that, they did not attempt to oppose him. His deeds had surrounded him with a mantle of such brightness that they dared not question him. They looked upon him not as a mere man, now, but as something godlike.

They went straight down the bank of the stream, and as they went, the city grew in size and brightness before them. Certainly it was one of the chief assemblies of the Comanches, and all that mighty place must be stirring like a nest of hornets with the news of the terribly disgraceful reverse which had overtaken their comrades on this day. And Thunder Moon, riding first, found that his nearest companion was always lagging a little farther behind him than mere respect demanded. Plainly this terrible attempt was not to the taste of the braves. They had done enough. They did not wish to tempt Providence.

And then another thought grew up in the mind of Thunder Moon. Their numbers, indeed, were too small to give them security in the face of such numbers as were yonder; but their numbers were large enough to make it almost impossible for them to enter the place without being perceived at once. But suppose that one bold man were to get into the Comanche city?

A moment later, the great thought was clear in his mind as a shining light, and he had made up his mind. He dismounted straightway.

He said to them:

"Tarawa, who leans from the sky and watches over his people, the Cheyennes, by day and night, now has whispered to me that you are not needed any further in this work. Remain here. Keep the horses here in the shadow of these trees beside the river. I, Thunder Moon, am going on alone."

There was a breath of silence, and then the voice of Big River exclaimed: "Consider, brother! Sometimes a man is made blind by great fortune!"

"Have no fear for me," smiled Thunder Moon. "Tarawa leads me!"

And he turned his back upon them and started away.

He left his rifle with them. If he needed a gun, then the two revolvers which he carried would be defense enough, for all his fighting was apt to be at close range. There was a short hatchet and a knife, furthermore, at his belt, and he was prepared to take his chance in this fashion.

Chapter Thirty-one

An indentation of the river shore which he was following enabled him to look back and see the four companions sitting their horses immovably beneath the shadow of the trees. They had not stirred, as they watched him out of sight, and no doubt they felt that he was advancing to certain death. He could not help wondering with a grim smile whether they would be more interested in his return, or in his death which would give them so much the more spoil to divide among themselves. Which would it be?

His own heart was beating wildly, when the first streaks of light from the town began to stain the waters of the river, showing its yellow face. He crouched to examine what was before him; for when traveling toward a light, it is better to look from beneath upward, always. He could see nothing except startlingly lifelike forms of shrubs, before him. At any moment, Comanches might start up from behind these shrubs. And yet he trusted that their last thought would be of so small a band daring to steal in upon the city! They would be searching in the distance for the thing that had stung them, and while they looked far off, perhaps he could blind them with a greater pain!

As these thoughts crossed his mind, he was aware of a sliding shadow passing him on the river surface, and he whirled, gun at hip. in time to see a long. heavy log—the trunk of a tree from which the branches had been chafed away float on downstream. Thunder Moon did not wait. He waded into the water until it was chest high, and then holding the holsters of his guns with his teeth, his head raised high, he swam out to the trunk and gripped the stub of one of the smaller, broken branches. On the trunk itself he placed his two guns, and now he floated down toward the lights of the town, far more swiftly than he had imagined the current was running.

All along the right bank, the lodges of the Comanches were pitched. and now the shafts of red light from their fires stained the surface of the water before him. He had a vague desire to abandon the trunk and swim hastily for the shore, but he conquered that impulse, and looking to the clear, starry face of the heavens, his heart was quieted. Whether he were to die, presently, or to achieve some great deed this night, was all in the hands of Tarawa!

In the meantime, he began to draw off his soaked clothes. When he was stripped to his loin cloth, he let the clothes sink in a knot in the river. But now he was free, except for the belt around his hips, and let the Comanches beware of this naked snake that was slipping down through the night to poison their lives!

The water was warm, his heart was momentarily lighter, and a strange, rich confidence flooded through his soul. Voices began to sound before him, and then a chorus of strong wailing.

Thunder Moon laughed cruelly. He knew for what cause the women of the Comanches were cutting off their hair, and gashing their bodies, and making this lament! Eleven lodges were desolate already!

And now straight past the edge of the camp he floated. Over him poured a flood of light from a great fire, and watching the shore, he saw the leaping flames, and around it an endless procession of warriors in the war dance.

He passed on. The whole community was in an uproar. And certainly among the ten who were dead, there must be the bodies of some famous men! That thought gave him the greater strength for the work which lay before him.

Presently, the log grounded with a jar, and the up-stream end swayed slowly inward. Along it he worked his way. To his right, the flames from the fire were staining the sky, and throwing huge, uncertain waves of illumination among the tepees, but near him, he could not see a soul. All seemed deserted, and the inhabitants had been drawn away to the war dance which promised revenge, and to the lament for the dead Comanches.

He crept up the bank and peered into the door of the first lodge. Within, he could see the weapons of warriors, and the posts where the headdresses and the medicine bags were hung. But there was no deed for him, here.

He looked into another, and another. In the third, a child lay crowing beside the fire, deserted by its mother. Some Cheyennes would instantly have buried their knives in its heart, and Thunder Moon wondered why there was nothing but horror in his own, at such a thought. Somewhere in him there was a vital weakness. It kept him from taking scalps. It made torture and cruelty horrible to him. And he was bitterly ashamed of these failings. He could only pray to Tarawa to reward him with some chance for a truly great service on this night to make up for the things which he could never be.

But here, on the outskirts of the city of tepees, how could he hope to find a chance for great deeds? No, the inner circle where the big lodges were must be his place.

And he turned with a beating heart to worm his way nearer to the heart of the Comanche town.

Near enough, at last, with the roar of voices from the dance beating in waves against his ears and confusing his brain, he selected the very largest of the lodges, and made toward it. He glanced through the open flap, and instantly he saw that his deed lay before him.

For just before him, on the opposite side of the tepee, with the light of the fire playing over him, was the Yellow Man. Thunder Moon felt that he should have known by the size and the elaborately painted surface of this lodge that it was the house of the god. All that Comanche art could do to make it an honorable dwelling had been performed, and now Thunder Moon was looking at the little idol made of a richly glimmering yellow metal such as he could not recall having seen before. The figure sat cross-legged, and its fat, puckered face stared out toward Thunder Moon with a sort of malevolent calmness.

But he knew that this was the Yellow Man, that chief god to whom the Comanches had prayed for generations. He wondered why there were only two figures in the tent, and he understood, a moment later. For by his first glance at the two, he knew them to be men of importance, and before he had listened to a dozen words, he was aware that the chief medicine man and the war chief of this section of the Comanche nation sat here in consultation before the face of the Yellow Man. The wizard was dressed in full regalia, and presently he rose, and with shaking rattles, passed back and forth before the idol. He was masked with the skull of a mountain lion, and his body was hideously stained with red and black. But whatever were the words he murmured as he danced, he was not satisfied with the answer which the god put in his heart. Suddenly he stopped and said:

"I go out to see what the stars say, O Antelope Tail. When I come back, perhaps the Yellow Man will speak."

And he strode through the flap of the lodge, straight

upon the waiting knife of Thunder Moon. The latter
drove the blow home with a true aim, and caught the
body in his left arm as it collapsed, but a last sighing gasp
broke from the lips of the medicine man and that gasp,
perhaps, might reach the ears of the chief above the distant chanting of the dancers around the fire.

Thunder Moon waited, knife bare, tensed for another
stroke, but Antelope Tail did not appear; so he carried
the dead man to the side of the lodge and laid him down
there. A fine mustang, standing saddled near by, with a
war club at the saddlebow, snorted.

Thunder Moon went back, and peering through the
flap, he saw the war leader standing with hands raised toward the god; then he, too, his head bowed and his arms
crossed on his breast, backed slowly out of the lodge.

Thunder Moon had shrunk down to the earth. The
knife was poised in his hand to fly instantly at the heart of
the chief, but the latter, wrapped in his thoughts, strode
slowly away toward the fire, around which the black figures of men were leaping up and down. For the Yellow
Man had not yet spoken, and the dance must continue
until his word was known, even if three days passed in his
silence!

There would be no better chance than this:

Into the tepee leaped the son of Big Hard Face, and
there he paused for a moment, overwhelmed. For it
seemed to him that red fire had entered the fixed eyes of
the god. Superstitious dread paralyzed the youth, but he
shook it off and drew a deep breath.

Yonder hung the medicine arrows, sacred to the tribe,
and here was their chief god. If he were stronger than the
Sky People who had helped Thunder Moon on this day,
let him stretch forth his hand and strike!

He gripped the image and lifted it.

He thought, at first, that it was taking on life and wriggling from his hands; but it was only the smoothness of
the metal and its singular weight. Tiny as it was, it made a
fifty or sixty-pound burden in the fingers of Thunder
Moon.

Under one arm he held it. The sacred arrows were

slung across his back, and catching up a robe, to wrap around the glimmering metal of the idol, lest the shining of it betray him, he stepped hastily outside.

Straight before him, and not fifty steps away, came the tall and solemn form of Antelope Tail, striding toward the house of the god again, to beg for an answer which would free him to take the warpath at once.

His head was bowed, his step was solemn.

But the racing heart of Thunder Moon had not beat five times, before he was in the saddle on the pony behind the medicine lodge, and the image in a saddle pouch, while he cast the buffalo robe over his shoulders, and gave the pony its head to race away through the tepees.

Why did they not know what had happened the instant that he started? Why did not the god tell these blind Comanches?

Then, behind Thunder Moon, a terrible cry went up through the night.

Now let all the Cheyenne gods defend you, Thunder Moon!

Chapter Thirty-two

He had headed the pony upstream, through the city; and now, as he broke from the last circle of the lodges, he saw its swift current, streaked red by the lights from the fires. He galloped like mad up the bank of the stream.

Every second before the pursuit should start was worth lifeblood! And now they came! An Indian's knife is hardly more ready to his hand than his horse, and the Comanches lived by their ponies.

Not half a dozen words had been needed to tell them what had happened, and they flooded out, maddened, bewildered, savage for blood!

Thunder Moon looked back. He could see five hundred forms in a dense mass racing behind him, and their screaming voices shot dread through his body. He felt weak with the greatness of the terrible thing that he had done. He felt the hand of the yellow god on his shoulder, drawing him back.

In the meantime, the narrow river lay between him and his friends and his fleet chestnuts on the farther bank. The god would slay him if he ventured to keep the sacred image any longer. He veered the pony straight into the water, and from the bank made it leap far out. They fell with a crash, rose to the surface, and Thunder Moon caught at the Yellow Man in the saddlebag. One arm of the little figure was broken off short by his grip. He reached again, took the idol by the head, and dropped it into the swift river, then forced the lightened horse on toward the white face of a rock on the opposite bank.

There was only a moment of swimming before the feet of the war pony touched bottom, but in that moment, the horde of swift riders had poured far up the bank of the river, and as Thunder Moon rode up the bank of the stream on the side of his companions, fifty guns spoke, and fifty war bows clanged behind him. Something like the edge of a knife slid across the left side of his face. A bullet grazed the top of his head. From both wounds, the blood flowed freely, and still, he was not seriously injured.

He turned in the saddle, to see the front ranks of the Comanches rush their horses at the water.

There was no use wasting time firing. For every man he might kill, there were a hundred braves maddened by religious fury and bloodlust ready to take his place, and Thunder Moon leaned forward in the saddle and devoted all his efforts to bettering the pace of the little horse.

It was a staunch pony, and yet the weight of its rider was great in the saddle, and as soon as the Comanches had crossed the stream, they began to gain rapidly on him. Looking back, he could see the pursuit drawing into a head, like the point of a lance, as the fastest horses gained the lead, and the rest of the Comanches followed as fast as they could. And as he looked ahead, marking the distance to the trees under which he had left his friends, he knew that he could never gain them in time.

Moreover, was it to be expected that they would even wait for him when they saw this great horde of enemies thundering toward them?

His despair turned to acute agony. For around a bend of the river before him came several charging horsemen. And now all retreat was cut off!

However, his revolvers were ready and perhaps, even in the dimness of the starlight, he could blast his way through the riders just before him.

He poised a gun in either hand. With a thrust of his heel, he sent the pony forward with racing speed. And then a familiar shout before him struck him to the heart with wonder and with joy.

It was the voice of Yellow Wolf, calling. Aye, and the horses had legs too long to be Indian ponies. Those were his men. They had not shrunk from the danger. For his sake, they had rushed forward to meet it, and out of the soul of Thunder Moon there arose a great silent hymn of thanksgiving that Tarawa could have placed such warriors upon earth and given them to him for companions and for brothers!

He shouted his answer with a ringing voice, and like so many birds wheeling in the wind, the troop of Cheyennes turned and fled up the river again. He was among them, already loose in the saddle.

Young Hawk, leaned from the back of his own horse, threw the lead rope of Sunset to their chief. And Thunder Moon leaped tigerlike to the back of his great horse, while the Comanche pony, lightened of its burdensome load sprang lightly ahead of the other riders.

One backward glance showed Thunder Moon the nearness of the flying Comanche peril. He saw it, and he set his teeth. For now, if they had magic horses, let their speed be shown for the sake of their dead medicine man, their captured arrows, and their lost god. Let them match strides against the long-legged chestnuts and the gods of Thunder Moon!

Aye, the medicine of the Comanches was weak indeed. Not a minute passed before a despairing wail arose from the following host as they saw their quarry disappearing in the night before them. And every stride carried Thunder Moon and his men closer to safety, while he shouted to them:

"There is nothing to fear. Their god is choked in the mud of the river-bottom! Their medicine arrows rattle on my shoulders. Their medicine man himself lies dead in their city. They are now like blind dogs, and their throats are offered to Cheyenne knives!"

And a screech of exulation rose from the throats of his companions. Such things were to be dreamed of, hardly to be believed!

There was nothing, after that, that really mattered, though there is much that could be told, and when the lodges of the Cheyennes were reached, at last, the companions of Thunder Moon did not dwell least upon the flight from the land of their enemies. For they were glad to tell how the first pursuit failed, and how, in the morning, they saw the white signals smoking in the sky behind them, and how a second band of Comanches rode across their way and were eluded in a stirring chase. And then, when the chestnuts were tired and gaunt, still a third great war party came full upon them. But the care which Thunder Moon had taken of his horses proved its worth, and even the third challenge was beaten off.

Weary—very weary—but yet light-hearted with joy, the Cheyennes saw the peaked tops of their lodges rising before them, at last, and the great war trail was ended.

And who could shake his head at Thunder Moon from that time forth because no scalps dried in his lodge? Not even Big Hard Face, hard as he was to please. For when he had such thoughts, he raised his head, and he looked at the medicine arrows of the Comanches hanging in his tepee, blackening in the smoke, growing brittle with misuse, as the fortunes of the Comanche nation would surely grow brittle also!

M